The stranger fumbled to flip on the light switch.

"Help!" Elizabeth shouted.

To her surprise, he looked more shocked than she felt. "What do you want?" she yelled.

Elizabeth's senses were fully alive in these fast-moving seconds, telling her more than her mind could take in. *Something is wrong, something is different.* The room was arranged the same, but the coloring was all wrong.

"Sarah, listen to me—"

"Why are you calling me that?" Elizabeth cried.

What was going on? Had she come out of the tub in some sort of sleepwalking trance, and wandered into someone else's house? Had she hit her head on the tub and, even now, was dreaming . . . in a coma . . . drowning?

She turned toward the stranger, who watched her anxiously. "Where am I? Who are you?"

Sudden Switch

Paul McCusker

LION
PUBLISHING

Lion Publishing
A Division of Cook Communications
4050 Lee Vance View
Colorado Springs, CO 80918, USA

SUDDEN SWITCH
© 1996 by Paul McCusker

First edition 1996

Cover design by Bill Paetzold
Cover illustration by Matthew Archambault

ISBN 0-7459-3611-3

Printed and bound in the United States of America
00 99 98 97 96   5 4 3 2 1

Published in association with the literary agency of Alive Communications, Inc., 1465 Kelly Johnson Blvd., Suite 320, Colorado Springs, CO 80920

Library of Congress Cataloging-in-Publication Data

McCusker, Paul
        Sudden switch / by Paul McCusker.
                p.   cm. — (Time twists)
        Summary: Fifteen-year-old Elizabeth suddenly finds herself in a
        parallel world where she is called Sarah and is diagnosed as
        having amnesia, while the real Sarah has taken Elizabeth's place
        and is in a coma.
                ISBN 0-7459-3611-3
                [1. Space and time—Fiction. 2. Identity—Fiction. 3.
        Christian life—Fiction.] I. Title. II. Series: McCusker, Paul, 1958-
        Time twists.
        PZ7.M47841635Sv   1996
        [Fic]—dc20   96-19911
                                                                   CIP
                                                                   AC

Dedicated with deepest love
to the real Elizabeth Sarah

and to Buddy Owens for coming up with the missing piece

Can a mortal ask questions which God finds unanswerable? Quite easily, I should think. All nonsense questions are unanswerable. How many hours are there in a mile? Is yellow square or round? Probably half the questions we ask—half our great theological and metaphysical problems—are like that.

C. S. Lewis, *A Grief Observed*

It is probable that Nature is not really in Time and almost certain that God is not. Time is probably (like perspective) the mode of our perception. There is therefore in reality no question of God's at one point in time (the moment of creation) adapting the material history of this universe in advance to free acts which you or I are to perform at a later point in Time. To Him all the physical events and all the human acts are present in an eternal Now.

C. S. Lewis, *Miracles*

"I'm running away," Elizabeth announced. Defiantly she chomped a french fry in half.

Jeff looked up at her from the malted milkshake in which he'd been absentmindedly swirling his straw while she complained about her parents—for the past half hour. "You're what?"

"You weren't listening, were you?"

"I was, too."

"Then what did I say?" Elizabeth tucked a loose strand of her long brown hair behind her ear so it wouldn't fall into the puddle of ketchup next to her fries.

"You were complaining about how your mom and dad drive you crazy and . . . your dad embarrassed you last night while you and Melissa Morgan were doing your history homework. And your dad lectured you for twenty minutes about . . . about . . ."

"Christian symbolism in the King Arthur legends," Elizabeth filled in.

"Yeah, except that you and Melissa were supposed to be studying the . . . um . . ."

"French Revolution."

"Right, and Melissa finally made up an excuse to go home, and you were embarrassed and mad at your dad—"

"*As usual,*" she said and savaged another french fry.

Jeff gave a sigh of relief. Elizabeth's pop quizzes were a lot tougher than anything they gave him at school. But it was hard for him to listen when she launched into another round about her parents. Not having any parents of his own, Jeff struggled to connect when Elizabeth went on and on about hers.

"Then what did I say?" she asked.

He was mid-suck on the straw and nearly blew the contents back into the glass. "Huh?"

"What did I say after that?"

"You said . . . uh . . ." He coughed, then glanced around the

Fawlt Line Diner, hoping for inspiration. The place was a tribute to days gone by, with its dazzling array of fluorescent lights, beveled mirrors, rippled chrome trim, worn red upholstery, and checkered floor tiles. And it boasted Alice Dempsey, the world's oldest living waitress, who now stood at their booth in her paper cap and red striped uniform with white apron.

Alice chewed her gum loudly and smelled like burnt hamburgers. "You kids want anything else?"

Rescued, Jeff thought. "No, thank you," he said out loud.

"See you tomorrow," Alice said. She cracked an internal bubble on her gum and dropped the check on the edge of the table.

"No, you won't," Elizabeth said under her breath. "I won't be here."

Alice shot a curious look back at Elizabeth as she walked off.

"You weren't listening," Elizabeth rebuked him. "I said I'm going to run away."

"Aw, c'mon, Bits—" Jeff had called Elizabeth "Bits" for as long as either of them could remember, which would be the ten years since she was five and he was six. "It's not that bad."

"You try living with my mom and dad, and tell me it's not that bad."

"I know your folks," Jeff said. "They're a little quirky, that's all."

"Quirky! They're just plain weird. They're clueless about life in the real world. All my dad knows are his books and his garden and his crazy ideas. Did you know that he went to church last Sunday with his shirt on inside out?"

"It happens."

"And wearing his *bedroom slippers*?"

Yeah, that's Alan Forde, all right, Jeff thought and stopped a smile before it got to his lips.

"And they're grass stained. Do you know why? Because my dad does his gardening in his bedroom slippers. He doesn't care. He doesn't care how he looks, what people think of him, or *anything*! And my mom doesn't even have the decency to be embarrassed for him. She thinks it's funny! They're weird."

"They're just . . . *themselves*. They're—"

Elizabeth threw herself against the back of the red vinyl bench and groaned. "You don't understand."

"Sure I do!" Jeff said. "Your parents are no worse than my Uncle Malcolm." Malcolm Dubbs, Jeff's father's brother, had been Jeff's guardian since his parents had died two years ago in a plane crash.

"They're much worse. Uncle Malcolm is nice and sensitive and . . ." Elizabeth's voice trailed off. "My parents just go on and on about things I don't care about. And if I hear the life-can't-be-taken-too-seriously-because-it's-just-a-small-part-of-a-bigger-picture lecture one more time, I'll go out of my mind."

Again Jeff restrained his smile. He knew that lecture well. Except Uncle Malcolm couched it in the phrase "eternal perspective." All it meant was that there was a lot more to life than what we can see or experience with our senses. As Uncle Malcolm said again and again, this world was a temporary stop on a journey to a truer, more *real* reality—an *eternal* reality. "They just look at things differently from most people," Jeff said, determined not to turn the gripe session into an Olympic event.

"They're from another planet. They're weird," Elizabeth repeated. "This whole town is weird. Haven't you figured it out yet?"

"I like Fawlt Line," Jeff said softly, afraid Elizabeth's complaints might offend some of the other regulars at the diner.

"Everybody's so . . . so *oblivious*! Nobody even seems to notice how strange this place is."

Jeff shrugged. "It's just a town, Bits. Every town has its quirks."

"Is that your word of the day?" Elizabeth snapped. "These aren't just *quirks*, Jeffrey."

Jeff sighed. When she resorted to calling him Jeffrey, there was no reasoning with her. He rubbed the side of his face and absentmindedly pushed his fingers through his wavy black hair.

"For instance, what about Helen?" Elizabeth challenged him.

"Which Helen? You mean our information operator? That Helen?"

"I mean our information operator who thinks she's psychic." Elizabeth leaned over the Formica tabletop. Jeff moved her plate of fries and ketchup to one side. "She won't let you off the phone until she guesses who you're trying to call. And she's never right!"

"Beats a recording like they have in the big towns."

"But doesn't it seem just a *little* bit nuts? I mean it, Jeff. This place is crazy. Our only life insurance agent has been dead for six years!"

"Yeah, but—"

"And don't forget Walter Keenan. He wanders the streets proofreading park bench ads!" Her voice was a shrill whisper.

"Ben Hearn only pays him to do that because he feels sorry for him. You know old Walter hasn't been the same since he got struck by lightning."

"Those are just a couple of examples," Elizabeth said, then sighed. "It's like Mayberry trapped in the Twilight Zone. I thought you'd understand. I thought you knew how nuts this town is."

Elizabeth locked her gaze onto Jeff's. Suddenly the image of her large brown eyes, the faint freckles on her upturned nose, and her full lips made him want to kiss her. He wasn't sure why— they'd been friends for so long that she'd probably laugh at him if he ever actually did it—but the urge was still there.

"It's not such a bad place," he managed to say.

Elizabeth shook her head. "I've had enough of this town and of my parents and of all the weirdness. I'm fifteen years old, and I wanna be a normal kid with normal problems. Are you coming with me or not?"

Jeff cocked an eyebrow. "Going with you where?"

"To wherever I run away to," she replied. "I'm serious about this, Jeff. I'm getting all my money together and going somewhere normal. We can take your Volkswagen and—"

"Listen, Bits, " Jeff interrupted, "I know how you feel. But we can't just run away. Where would we go? What would we do?"

"Who are you all of a sudden: Mr. Responsibility? You never know where you're going or what you're doing. Mr. Vidler says you're just like Huck Finn."

"Mr. Vidler said that?" Jeff asked defensively, wondering why their English teacher would be talking about him to Elizabeth.

"He says it's because you don't have parents, and your Uncle Malcolm doesn't care what you do."

Jeff grunted. He didn't like the idea of Mr. Vidler discussing his family like that.

Elizabeth continued, "So why should you care where we go or what we do? Let's just get out of here."

"But, Bits—"

"No! I'm not listening to you!" Elizabeth shouted and hit the table top with the palms of her hands. Silence washed over the diner like a wave as everyone turned to look.

"Keep it down, will you?" Jeff whispered fiercely.

Elizabeth dropped her voice. "Either you go with me, or stay here and rot in this town. It's up to you."

Jeff looked away. He and Elizabeth never argued, and he didn't like it. Eventually he shrugged. "I don't know."

Elizabeth softened her tone. "If you're going, then meet me at the Old Sawmill by the edge of the river at ten." She paused, then added, "I'm going whether you come with me or not."

CHAPTER 2

Jeff lived with his Uncle Malcolm in a cottage where the north edge of town connected with the south edge of the Dubbs family estate. The estate, owned by the Dubbses since the 1700s, included hundreds of acres of forest and rolling hills. It had a mansion, too, but nobody lived there. Though he was the master of the Dubbs family fortune, Malcolm chose to live modestly in the cottage. Without a wife or children, he reasoned, he didn't need to live in the "big house." Besides, he liked the coziness of the cottage, and thought it suited him perfectly. Jeff had joined him there right after his parents died.

Uncle Malcolm, tall and lean, was hunched like a weeping willow over the large desk in his den when Jeff slipped in to see him. The sun had set, and a single banker's lamp illuminated the desktop with a greenish glow. The slight flicker from a neglected mound of hot coals in the fireplace cast stark shadows that danced around the cluttered room with its old-fashioned furniture, dark wood paneling, shelves spilling over with books, and paintings and drawings thrown randomly on the walls.

The clock on the mantelpiece struck the quarter hour.

"Uncle Malcolm?"

"It's not right, Jeff," Uncle Malcolm said. "It's still not right. Come look."

Jeff crossed the room, knowing full well what Uncle Malcolm was pondering. On his desk were the plans for his "Time Village"—a theme park dedicated to history. Uncle Malcolm was determined to use the Dubbs family's vast estate to bring in homes, farms, and buildings brick by brick from all over the world. Each one would capture as accurately as possible a different period of history. Uncle Malcolm had all the money and resources he needed to pull the scheme off.

Pointing to the left side of the drawing where someone had roughly sketched in a cluster of houses, Uncle Malcolm asked,

14

"Do you think it makes sense to put the mining village of the 1850s right next to the 1790 French farmhouse?"

Jeff looked closely at the plans and said, "It makes about as much sense as putting that New England schoolhouse from 1908 next to the blacksmith shop from 1672."

"Exactly! It makes no sense at all!" Uncle Malcolm clapped Jeff on the back and smiled at him with bright blue eyes that always reminded Jeff of his father. "You're thinking the same way I am. People should come into the village and move from point to point chronologically! That way they see the growth and develop-ment of civilization."

Jeff nodded.

Uncle Malcolm folded his arms. "I'll just tell that confounded contractor that I don't care how much it costs to redo the land-scape. If we're going to build this village, we have to build it right."

"Right," Jeff agreed.

Uncle Malcolm turned his chair away from the plans to face Jeff. "And what can I do for you, my boy? I know you didn't come in here to listen to me rattle on about my village."

"I kind of have a problem," Jeff said.

Uncle Malcolm's eyebrows arched. "Really? Then you'd bet-ter sit down."

As Jeff slid into the cushioned embrace of one of the thick wingback chairs, he thought of how much he depended on his uncle. He knew there were some folks in town who thought Malcolm Dubbs was a little off-the-wall and maybe even unsuit-able to raise a child. "He lets the boy run wild," Jeff had once overheard Mrs. Gardner at the grocery store say. Maybe it was true. But Jeff couldn't imagine a better substitute for the parents who could never be replaced.

He self-consciously fingered the growing hole in the left leg of his jeans, then said, "It's Elizabeth. She wants to run away."

"To where?"

Jeff shrugged. "I don't know. She says her parents are driving her crazy and she wants to live somewhere normal."

"And I suppose she wants you to run away with her."

"How did you know?"

"You've been friends an awful long time. It makes sense that she'd want your help."

Jeff shook his head. "She's not asking for my help. She doesn't want anybody's help."

"I suspect you're wrong," Uncle Malcolm said. "Elizabeth likes people to think she's independent, but she needs other people just as you or I do. That's why she wants you to run away with her. To give her support and advice." He paused and tugged at his ear as he often did when he was thinking. "Well, are you going to do it?"

Jeff was startled. "What?"

"Are you going to run away with Elizabeth?" his uncle asked, as if it were a very reasonable course of action.

Jeff smiled to himself. This was the attitude of Uncle Malcolm's that made Mrs. Gardner and her kind crazy. "You're joking, right? I couldn't run away with her."

"Why not?"

Jeff needed a moment to think it over. "Well, I know she doesn't have much money. And I sure don't have any, except for my trust fund." He couldn't touch that till he was twenty-one. "So I don't know where we'd go or what we'd do or how we'd survive."

Uncle Malcolm nodded. "Anything else?"

Jeff figured he had covered it all, but he thought another moment. Then he frowned. "To be honest, I have to be sensible. I understand her wanting to run away, but I think she's running from one problem to a whole bunch of new ones."

Uncle Malcolm smiled. "You're a smart lad. And what you just told me, you have to tell her."

"She won't listen."

"You're her closest friend. If she won't listen to you, she won't listen to anybody," Uncle Malcolm said. "When is she planning to go?"

"I'm supposed to meet her at the Old Sawmill at ten o'clock."

"Then meet her—and make her see how unprepared she is to run away. Help her work out a plan."

"A plan for what?"

"To run away, of course—once she's saved her money, established where she'll go, and determined how she'll live once she gets there."

"But it'll take years for her to figure all that out."

"Exactly. Long enough for her to see how silly it is to run off. Maybe it'll give her time to realize how much her parents love her—even if they do drive her crazy. Nobody's perfect."

"You are."

"Don't be ridiculous. It just seems that way because I'm not a parent." Uncle Malcolm laughed. "Now, don't forget that I'm leaving tomorrow for Washington, D. C. I'm not sure how long I'll be gone, but Mrs. Packer will know how to get in touch with me. Let her know if you need anything."

Mrs. Packer was their housekeeper.

"Okay, Uncle Malcolm," Jeff said. "Thanks."

"Don't thank me; you're the one who came up with the answers. You just needed a little help to recognize them."

The chair creaked as Jeff stood up.

As if it were an afterthought, Uncle Malcolm added, "Oh, and if Elizabeth won't listen to reason, just tie her up and drag her home until she comes to her senses."

"Yes, sir." Jeff grinned and walked to the door. As he reached for the knob, he suddenly turned back. "Do you think I'm like Huck Finn, Uncle Malcolm?"

"Heavens, no! You're a lot more intelligent than Huck Finn. Why do you ask?"

"Just wondering," Jeff said and closed the door behind him.

CHAPTER 3

The funny thing was: Elizabeth didn't want to take a bath in the first place. But it seemed to be the only refuge for her frayed nerves. She was angry with Jeff for not agreeing wholeheartedly to run away with her. And once she returned to the Victorian house she called home, her folks seemed unusually attentive to her, as if they knew she was up to something. *It's that old "parents' radar" again,* she thought. *Somehow they know when they're not wanted and insist on staying close by.*

Her father, who normally besieged her with his latest discovery in the garden or a Greek phrase he had translated from an old manuscript, had apparently decided that tonight was the time to ask about her day at school.

Then her mother said she'd heard that Elizabeth and Jeff had had some sort of quarrel at the diner. How had that news reached home even before she did? Small towns were unbelievable . . . and Fawlt Line was surely among the worst. Her mother was concerned—she knew Elizabeth and Jeff never quarreled. Was everything all right, she wanted to know. Elizabeth mumbled a vague response and excused herself to go to her room.

She was looking in her closet for good running-away clothes when her mother came in. More questions. "Are you feeling all right? Are you sure you don't want to talk about what happened with Jeff? You seem unhappy about something, Elizabeth. What is it?"

Elizabeth ran out of evasive answers and finally announced that she was going to take a bath. It was the only escape; the only reprieve for her tense muscles and tangled emotions.

As she stepped into the bathroom that adjoined her bedroom, Elizabeth turned to glance at her mother. Jane Forde stood in the center of the bedroom, a worried expression on her face, her hands knotted. The muted yellow light of the bedside lamp made her look old.

18

"Your father and I have a meeting at church. We'll be back in an hour or so."

"Okay, Mom." Elizabeth closed the door and turned the key in the lock.

Her robe, its limp arms dangling in a gesture of resignation, hung carelessly from a hook on the white wooden door. Elizabeth spun the chrome clover-shaped faucet handles. The spigot spat, the pipes groaned, and the water roared into the milky-white claw-footed tub. She wiggled her fingers under the waterfall to test the temperature, then pinned her hair up into a bun. She considered peeking to see if her mother was still in her room, but decided against it. It would only trigger more questions.

Cautiously she touched a toe to the water. Not too hot, not too cold—just right, like the littlest bear's porridge. She stepped into the tub and sat down, stretching her long legs as far as possible. The tub was too short and made bald islands of her knees. She put her head back, and the steam rose around her. The water licked at the bottom of her chin. Her body was prickly velvet. She closed her eyes and let her thoughts run.

Jeff wouldn't meet her at the Old Sawmill. He wouldn't run away. Why should he? He didn't have weird parents who embarrassed him. He didn't know what it was like.

She looked across the still bath water. Though she hadn't moved, the water suddenly rippled as if someone had tapped the side of the tub with a tack-hammer. It settled again. She pushed a stray lock of hair away from her eyes and slid deeper into the water.

He probably went home and talked to his uncle, her inner thoughts continued. *Uncle Malcolm would talk him out of running away even if he wanted to go. He'd show Jeff that it wasn't smart, without any money or any plan. How would they survive?*

Well, how did anyone ever survive? She and Jeff didn't need a plan. They'd figure it out as they went along. And making money should be easy enough. There were plenty of odd jobs for kids to do.

But—

There was a still, small voice in the back of her mind. *Be honest*, it said. She squeezed her eyes closed, hoping to block the voice out, but it demanded to be heard.

You don't know the first thing about surviving. You don't know how to make any money. Your parents have always given you an allowance. Where will you go? What will you do? What's so terrible about your life that you want to run away?

You don't know, she answered the voice. *You don't understand.*

I know, the voice said. *I understand.*

Her internal argument made her feel tense again. She lifted up her right foot just as a drop of water fell from the tap. It splashed cold against her skin. She sighed and closed her eyes.

Was the voice right? Was her life really so bad? Would running away only take her out of the frying pan into the fire? The first cracks of doubt appeared on the surface of her determination. Did she really know what she was getting herself into?

Suddenly rough hands grabbed her, hard fingers grasped her throat, pressing tight, pushing her under icy water.

Elizabeth gasped and opened her eyes. She glanced around. The bathroom was as it had been: stark and untroubled.

Where in the world did that come from? she wondered. She tried to reconstruct the image in her mind, but it was a blur. Rough hands around her throat. No air. No breath.

How bizarre, she thought as she tried to calm down. She didn't usually have violent thoughts or imaginings, regardless of how tense she felt. *I'm just upset,* she concluded. She glanced down into the bath and instantly recoiled.

The water was filthy brown with bits of grass and sludge floating on top, as if a sewer had backed up through the drain. Her stomach turned, and she grabbed the sides of the tub to pull herself out. She pushed but couldn't get her footing on the slick porcelain. Her legs splayed out and she lost her grip, sending her body splashing downward, sliding toward the front of the tub. Her head dipped under the water and hit against the bottom. She thrashed out, her hands clawing at something, anything. She grabbed the edge, pulling herself up with all her strength, and catapulted herself over the side of the tub. The water spilled with her as she struck the cold tiled floor. She lay on her side, coughing and sputtering for a moment. She wanted to scream for her dad, but she couldn't find the breath.

What happened? How could—? Her mind was tangled with the impossibility of what had happened.

She got her breathing under control and sat up. Her hip protested by sending a sharp pain down her leg. She examined it closely. *That'll be a doozy of a bruise by morning.* She peered into the tub for a look at the water. It was gone. The tub was bone dry.

A dream. I must've fallen asleep in the bath and slipped under the water. Of course. I let the water out. I've been lying here for a long time. It's the only thing that makes sense.

On unsteady legs she stood up to dry herself. The pain in her side was already fading. She dropped the towel on the floor and pushed it around with her foot to mop up the puddles she'd made. She nearly laughed out loud. *What will Jeff say when I tell him about this?* He'd probably scold her for falling asleep in the bath. Maybe he'd make a joke about how dirty she was.

Still, the violent image of rough hands strangling her flashed in and out of her mind like a flickering strobe. Rough hands, the strangling feeling, brown water.

She turned to the small shelf above the toilet tank where she had placed a pair of clean panties and a T-shirt. They weren't there. *That's funny*, she thought. *I'm sure I brought some in.* She must've left them in the bedroom. She reached for the robe hanging on the door, but it was gone, too.

Wait a minute, she said to herself. *I may have forgotten my T-shirt and panties, but I know the robe was there.* Suddenly, she was unsure of herself. *Am I dreaming?*

She opened the door, wondering if her mom was still there. The bedroom was dark.

Light spilled in from the bathroom, guiding her as she made

her way to the dresser. She opened the top drawer and retrieved some panties. The T-shirt was next. In the closet, she found a robe, but it was unfamiliar to her. Probably one of her mother's resale shop finds. She put it on.

The house was strangely quiet. She sat down on the edge of the bed, trying to pinpoint why she felt so odd. A leftover feeling from what happened in the tub, perhaps.

She heard footsteps in the hall, and her skin went goose-pimply. Her parents were supposed to be at church.

There was a shadow of feet under the door.

"Mom?" she whispered, surprised at how her voice caught in her throat.

The door slowly opened. Even by the dim light from the bath-room, she could make out the shape and shadowy details of the face.

It wasn't her mom. Or her dad.

Elizabeth put a hand to her mouth to stifle her cry even as the stranger glanced toward the bathroom, then suddenly snapped his head in her direction. His eyes grew wide.

They both screamed.

CHAPTER 4

The stranger fumbled to flip on the light switch.

Elizabeth grabbed a lamp from the bedstead to use as a weapon.

"Help!" she shouted.

The stranger was young, maybe sixteen, stocky, and wearing a white Oxford shirt and dark trousers. His face had a set square look, his eyes were wide with bewilderment, and his short blonde hair stuck out in several directions as if a comb of static had passed through it. He stretched out his arm in a silent appeal and his mouth moved, but no words came out.

To Elizabeth's surprise, he looked more shocked than she felt. "What do you want?!" she shouted.

"Want?" he asked softly. He seemed genuinely confused.

"I'll call the police!" She glanced down at the bedstead. The phone was gone.

Something is wrong, something is different.

Elizabeth's senses were fully alive in these fast-moving seconds, telling her more than her mind could take in. *Something is wrong, something is different.* The room was arranged the same, the placement of the bed and the dressers unchanged. But the coloring was all wrong. The curtains were a busier, darker pattern. The dressers were lighter, oak instead of the rich, red cherry that she loved.

Where were her parents? Had they really gone to church, or had this stranger knocked them out and dumped their bodies somewhere?

"Where're my parents?" she demanded. "What did you do with them?"

"Your parents?" the stranger asked. "Sarah! What's the matter with you?"

"Sarah?! Nothing's wrong with *me*, bud. But you'll have plenty to tell the police!" She raised the lamp high and moved to the foot of the bed. If she could only get to the phone in her parents' room. *At least, I hope there's still a phone in my parents' room.*

"Sarah, listen to me—"

"Just stay where you are," she warned. The boy's arms were still outstretched, his palms turned upward in entreaty, but he took a couple of steps backward, as if to show that he wouldn't suddenly race for her.

As Elizabeth rounded the foot of the bed, the lamp's electrical cord reached its limit. The lamp leapt from her hand and crashed to the floor. With a loud pop, the bulb shattered and the light went out.

Elizabeth screamed and ran through the doorway into the hallway. Again, in an instant, she was aware of how different it seemed—like her home, and at the same time unlike. She banged into a small unfamiliar table with an equally unfamiliar potted plant on top. The plant tipped over, and a collection of framed photos scattered.

The strange boy peeked around the door frame, then appeared in the doorway. He didn't look threatening, nor did he come any closer. "Sarah, listen to me," he said calmly. "I don't understand what's going on. Why are you here? Are you playing some kind of game?"

"Stay away from me!" Elizabeth said.

From the bottom of the stairs a woman called out, "Calvin? Calvin, is everything all right?"

Startled, Elizabeth opened her mouth to scream for help, but before she could, the boy responded.

"Yeah, Mom! I'm just talking to Sarah," he called back.

"Is she back? I didn't hear her come in," the woman's voice replied.

He turned to Elizabeth again. "Sarah, please. Don't upset my parents again."

"Why are you calling me that?" Elizabeth snapped.

"What do you want me to call you?" he asked, then he squinted at her curiously. "Are you all right? I mean, you didn't hurt

24

yourself or anything, did you?"

"No!" she snarled. What was going on here? This boy—this Calvin—stood in the doorway as if . . . as if he *belonged* there. He didn't look threatened or worried . . . he looked perfectly at home.

"Maybe if we sit down and talk about it," he offered.

"Shut up!" Elizabeth cried, panicking. Why couldn't she sort out what was happening? Did she really believe that in the short time she was in the bath, this stranger had done away with her parents, redecorated her home, and brought in some woman to pretend to be his mother downstairs? It didn't make sense. Nothing made sense.

"I'm going to call the police," she said.

The boy stepped forward. "Do you want me to take you to the phone?" There was a teasing tone in his voice.

She growled at him, "Keep away from me. I don't know who you are or what you want, but *stay away!*" Her eyes darted about to see if there was anything within reach that might serve as a weapon, and landed on one of the tumbled photo frames.

Elizabeth held up the picture and stared at the tiny color photo inside the plain gold frame. She swallowed hard. It was a picture of the stranger sitting on a blanket in a large grassy field, with a picnic spread out nearby. He was holding up a glass as if making a toast. And sitting next to him, smiling happily was . . . she herself.

Gasping, she stepped back against the banister.

There was no denying it—there were the two of them in the same photo, sharing some happy memory on a picnic somewhere.

She swayed unsteadily, the photo moving in and out of focus.

What was going on? Had she come out of the tub in some sort of sleepwalking trance, and wandered into someone else's house? Had she hit her head on the tub and, even now, was dreaming . . . in a coma . . . drowning?

She put a hand to her head and turned toward the stranger, who watched her anxiously. "Where am I? Who are you?"

"I don't understand," he said. "You really don't know, do you?"

"I wouldn't ask if I knew!"

He raised his hands compliantly. "All right. Okay, I'll play along. My name is Calvin Collins."

Elizabeth reached behind her to grab the banister for support. "Calvin Collins," she repeated. The name meant nothing to her.

"Yeah. You know," he said, watching her carefully. "I'm your boyfriend."

Elizabeth slumped to the floor.

CHAPTER 5

"I'm losing my mind," Elizabeth whispered.

Calvin stooped next to her. He reached out to touch her shoulder, then apparently thought better of it and withdrew his hand. "What happened? Why are you acting like this?"

"I want my parents," she said. "I want Jeff." Her whole body was numb with shock. She looked Calvin full in the face, but couldn't manage to say anything else. Where should she start? How could she frame the question that would make sense of what had happened to her?

"Maybe I should take you to the hospital," Calvin said softly. "I don't know what's going on, but you're making me really nervous."

"*You're* nervous?!" she wanted to cry out. But instead she drew her knees up to her chest, wrapped her arms around them, and began to rock. "Who am I? Where am I?"

"You're Sarah Bishop. Who do you think you are?"

She shook her head as if to say *No, I'll ask the questions now.* "Where am I?"

Calvin moved from his crouching position and sat on the worn carpet. "You're in my house—my parents' house. You moved in after your mom and dad . . ." He looked away uncomfortably. "After they were killed in a car accident. Don't you remember?"

How can I remember something that didn't happen? Or did it? Were her parents killed, and now she was deep in some kind of psychotic shock or denial? "I don't remember. It doesn't make sense. I took a bath, that's all. I took a bath, and when I came out, everything was different." Her voice sounded shrill to her ears, the way she imagined a voice would sound when a person was on the edge of a nervous breakdown.

"Maybe you fell in the tub and hit your head," Calvin suggested. "I've read about stuff like that. Maybe you have some kind of amnesia. Come on, let me take you to the hospital. You might be hurt really bad in ways we can't see."

Elizabeth nodded and rose unsteadily to her feet. "Okay. But I'd like to use your phone first. Maybe if I try to call my parents—"

"Your parents are dead!" Calvin blurted.

"Just let me try!" Elizabeth screamed.

He guided her into a room that Elizabeth realized should be her parents' bedroom. It even had the same tacky wallpaper with dull yellow flowers on a rose background. She fought back the tears as she picked up the receiver and dialed her home number. Hope rose deep within her as she heard the phone ring once . . . twice . . . three times . . . and then get picked up. Her heart felt as if it might burst.

"Hello?" said a tinny masculine voice, not her father's.

"May I speak with Alan or Jane Forde please?"

The voice sounded annoyed. "You have the wrong number." *Click.*

"Come on, Sarah," Calvin said gently.

Elizabeth clenched her teeth and dialed the number again. The same voice answered and hung up, even more annoyed at being bothered a second time. She slammed down the phone, then picked it up and dialed Jeff's number—Melissa's number—Karen's number—every number she could think of—bothering strangers at home or, in one case, a dry cleaning establishment.

Frantic now to connect with someone she knew—anyone— even Helen, the bogus psychic information operator—Elizabeth dialed and dialed. But she didn't know anyone and, worse, wasn't known by anyone. Finally Calvin took the phone from her hand and put his arm around her to guide her out of the room.

The tears burn as they spill from her eyes, and there's a howling in her ears that she recognizes as her own voice crying out . . . crying out into a darkness that sucks her swirling and spinning into it . . . until her body falls in slow motion just the way it would in the movies . . . into a darkness without relief, but she welcomes it anyway because she thinks the darkness will let her escape from this bizarre nightmare. . . .

But it doesn't.

CHAPTER 6

Alan Forde wasn't easily alarmed. But as he stood knocking on his daughter's bathroom door, it was definitely alarm that he felt. Elizabeth had started her bath before Alan and Jane left for church an hour and a half ago. There was no sign that she'd ever come out.

He knocked again. "Elizabeth!"

There was no answer apart from the soft echo of a drop of water hitting a tub already full. He rattled the handle and pushed on the door.

"What should we do?" his wife asked from behind him. "Should I call someone?"

"No," he said as he tried the handle again and threw his weight against the door. He had never thought of Elizabeth as the suicidal type. But she had been acting so strange all evening and maybe . . . maybe . . .

"Alan!" Jane sobbed.

Alan was an ox of a man, over six feet tall, 225 pounds of solid flesh and bone. He wasn't about to be defeated by a wooden door. He backed up and threw his shoulder against it again. And again. And again, until he heard the snap of the catch and the wrenching of the supporting screws. Once, then twice more and the door cracked and splintered and flew open. Alan, off-balance, nearly crashed to the bathroom floor. He grabbed the towel rack to steady himself.

"Elizabeth!"

Her T-shirt and panties were neatly folded on the shelf above the toilet. The shower curtain was drawn around the tub. *She fell asleep in the tub!* Alan thought. *Dear God, don't let her drown.* He threw the shower curtain aside with such force that it popped from several rings.

The tub was full of water—the spigot continued to drip indifferently—but Elizabeth wasn't there.

Jane put her hand to her mouth.

Alan reached down to feel the water. Cold. He stood up straight and put his hands on his hips. A locked door, an empty, windowless bathroom, cold water . . . *where was Elizabeth?*

His analytical mind flipped through the possibilities like so many index cards in a box. Jane raced from the bathroom. Alan could hear her screaming Elizabeth's name throughout the house.

Alan shook his head. *She's not here.* He knew without knowing how he knew. *She's gone.*

On feet that seemed somehow disconnected from the rest of his body, Alan walked to the phone on Elizabeth's bedside table. He wanted to believe that there was a simple explanation for all this. He sat down on the edge of her bed and searched through the debris of her untidiness. Beneath a half-read novel, a stained mug, and scattered note paper, he found her address book.

"Elizabeth!" his wife shouted frantically from the other end of the house.

Alan picked up the receiver and systematically called everyone in his daughter's address book. First her closest friends, then the names he didn't recognize. One by one they gave the same answer: no, they hadn't seen her.

A solitary tear slid from his eye, journeyed down the bridge of his nose, and fell to his grass-stained bedroom slipper.

Elizabeth sat numbly in the passenger seat of Calvin's compact car, watching the familiar lights of an unfamiliar city spin past. Calvin was talking, but she caught only snippets of what he said.

"Your name is Sarah . . . you're my girlfriend . . ."

"I want to go home," she said.

"We're almost at the hospital," Calvin said. He was quiet for a moment. "Don't you remember *anything*, Sarah?"

I took a bath, she wanted to explain. *That was all. I thought somebody grabbed me, tried to drown me. The water was dirty. I slipped and hit my head on the bottom of the tub. And when I came out, everything was different.* But she just shook her head.

"Tell me more about who you think you are," Calvin said.

"Elizabeth," she said sharply, hoping that the sound of her own voice saying her own name would bring her back to reality. "Elizabeth Forde. My mom and dad are Jane and Alan Forde . . ." It was all she could say. Panic and tears choked off the rest.

"It's all right," Calvin said calmly, but his voice betrayed his worry. "We'll get a doctor to look at you."

"I took a bath," she whispered, barely audible above the hum of the car motor. "Maybe I hit my head under the water."

Calvin looked at her as if startled by the revelation. "Maybe you did," he agreed. "A doctor will know."

But the doctor on duty at the emergency room *didn't* know, Elizabeth realized quickly. He grunted and probed, muttering that her scalp showed no sign of cuts, bruises, or swelling. "A slight bump on the back, but incidental," he observed to no one as his stiff hands moved around her skull. He checked the bones in her face. "You think you fell asleep in the tub? Maybe bumped your head, huh?"

"Maybe," Elizabeth answered. She knotted her hands in her lap, her fingers touching and twisting the leg of the cotton sweat pants she had on—Sarah's, just like the pullover sweater Calvin offered her. And the white socks and the sneakers. All a perfect fit.

The doctor—"Dr. Stewart," his badge said—grunted again, then went through the routine of checking her pupils. "Size . . . equality . . . reactivity . . . " he murmured. "No discoloration . . ." Her ears and nose were next, then her mouth. "No blood . . . no unusual fluids . . ."

With a nurse assisting, the doctor checked Elizabeth's neck and chest, abdomen, lower back, lower and upper extremities. He noted the bruise on the side of her leg, nodded and scribbled as she explained how she had slipped and fallen in the bathroom. Apart from the bruise, she felt no pain at all, only the awkward discomfort of having her body manhandled by a complete stranger.

"Once again, tell me everything," Dr. Stewart insisted.

Elizabeth chewed at her lower lip. She wasn't sure where to start—or how much to confess. Finally, she explained that she took a bath after her parents left for a meeting at church. She was planning to see Jeff a little later.

Dr. Stewart gestured to Calvin. "This is Jeff?"

"No," Elizabeth said.

"I'm *Calvin*," Calvin said, chagrined. "Her *boyfriend*."

Dr. Stewart mumbled to himself and scratched his chin with the top of his pen. "Then what?"

"In the bath I—" Elizabeth stopped, unsure how much to say about what she had imagined in the tub. *They're strangers. It's none of their business.* "I think I slipped and hit my head. I'm not sure."

Dr. Stewart waved his pen at Calvin. "You were in the house when she took her bath? You didn't hear anything?"

"I didn't know she was in the tub," Calvin replied. "I thought she was out and—"

"She went out?"

"Earlier, yeah," Calvin admitted reluctantly.

"With Jeff?" Dr. Stewart asked.

"I don't even know anybody named Jeff. She said she was

going to a movie by herself. She does it all the time. Maybe she took a bath when she got home. I don't know. I don't know anything except that I peeked into her room later and . . . and she was like this."

Elizabeth shook her head. "I hate to go to movies by myself. I had a bad day with my parents and took a bath to relax. Why can't I get anyone to believe me?"

"Who doesn't believe you?" Dr. Stewart asked.

Elizabeth looked at Calvin.

"Her parents are dead," Calvin muttered apologetically. "She tried to call all these people she claims to know, and they don't exist. I don't know why she can't snap out of it."

Elizabeth shook her head and looked away from Calvin.

"Let's see what some X-rays will tell us," Dr. Stewart said brightly.

CHAPTER 8

At the Old Sawmill, Jeff woke up with a start. He had fallen asleep in a corner where he had a clear view of the door. He didn't want to miss Elizabeth when she came in. He twitched his nose at the cobwebs and coughed at the overwhelming smell of rotten wood. Outside, he could hear the river splashing over the rocks.

He looked at his watch. Twenty-five past ten. Where was Elizabeth? Had she given up on her plan to run away? Then why hadn't she given him a call and spared him the trip?

He heard something outside and suddenly realized that it was the noise that had wakened him. It was a sound like a car door slamming shut.

He scrambled to his feet just as two uniformed police officers burst through the door, scouted the area, and raced toward him. He backed against the wall.

"Don't move," one of the officers commanded and roughly grabbed his arm.

Jeff yelped, but didn't struggle. "What's going on?" he asked.

A third man stepped through the door and frowned at the officer. "You don't have to manhandle him, Bill."

The officer immediately let go of Jeff's arm.

"You two check the area," the third man ordered. The officers obeyed, and the man in charge turned his attention to Jeff. "Hi, Jeff," he said. Jeff recognized him from photos in the newspaper. Richard Hounslow, Fawlt Line's new sheriff. He was a tall mountain of a man with a round, boyish face, wavy brown hair, and the kind of pleasant, no-nonsense attitude you'd expect from a small-town law officer. "Andy Griffith on steroids" was the way one of Jeff's friends had described him.

"What's wrong? Was I trespassing? I didn't see any signs," Jeff said guiltily.

"What're you doing out here?"

Jeff swallowed hard. "Well, I came out to . . . take a walk and then I got tired and thought I'd come in here and . . . and . . ." He didn't believe a word of it himself.

"You haven't seen Elizabeth Forde, have you?" Sheriff Hounslow asked.

"Elizabeth? No," he answered honestly. "Why?"

"She's missing, and we thought you might know about it."

"Missing!" His mind reeled as he tried to guess what kind of foolish thing Elizabeth might have done. Had she decided to run away on her own?

Sheriff Hounslow hooked his thumbs in his pockets. "Look, Jeff, there's no point in acting innocent. Alice Dempsey at the diner overheard you two talking about meeting out here tonight." He stopped and chuckled. "Though she thought you said you were going to Old *Sawyer's*."

Jeff rolled his eyes. Sawyer's was the name of the drugstore on Main Street. Leave it to Alice to mishear what she overheard.

"We figured it out," the sheriff said, growing serious again. "Where's Elizabeth?"

Jeff shrugged. "I don't know. I mean, it's true we were going to meet here. She was mad at her parents and wanted to run away. But I was planning to talk her out of it. Honest."

"So where is she?"

"I don't know. Did you check her house?"

"Her dad called us. That's what started this whole thing. Her folks are understandably very upset. Now why don't you come clean and tell me where she is?"

Jeff was worried. If she wasn't at home and hadn't come to meet him, then something *was* wrong. "I don't know," he insisted.

And he continued to insist all the way to the police station.

CHAPTER 9

"The X-rays are clean as a whistle," Dr. Stewart announced. "There's nothing here that would lead me to conclude that you've suffered any shock or injury. Now, I'm no neurologist—"

"Then who is? Get him," Calvin said with a scowl.

"We're a small hospital; we can't afford round-the-clock neurologists. You can try Uniontown, or you can come back tomorrow when Dr. Kennedy is here."

"Tomorrow?" said Elizabeth. Was it possible that she might still be in this strange situation tomorrow? *No. I'll be awake by tomorrow, and this nightmare will be over.*

Dr. Stewart rubbed his eyes wearily and spoke to Calvin. "It's up to you. I can admit her for the night for observation, but I don't think it'll make a difference. To be honest, I doubt if a neurologist can help her either."

"Then what am I supposed to do?" Elizabeth asked.

"Get a good night's sleep and come back tomorrow," Dr. Stewart answered as he scribbled on a pad.

"But you just said—"

"Not to see a neurologist," Dr. Stewart interrupted, tearing the paper from the pad and handing it to Calvin, "but to talk to Dr. Waite."

"Who's Dr. Waite?" Calvin asked.

"He works in the psychiatric wing," said Dr. Stewart carefully.

"I'm not crazy," said Elizabeth through clenched teeth.

Dr. Stewart smiled patiently. "Of course not. It's routine. Any time patients come in with a problem that can't be traced to a physical cause, we send them to the psychiatric wing for a look-over."

"A look-over for *what*?" Elizabeth demanded.

"For something other than a physical cause." Dr. Stewart turned to Calvin, his smile frozen in place. "See that she meets with Dr. Waite."

Calvin nodded silently.

Elizabeth pounded the diagnostic table. "He's not my keeper!"

"Look, I've done all I can," Dr. Stewart said, his voice showing the first crack in his pleasant exterior. "I'd love to try to figure this out for you but, frankly, I have emergencies waiting." He turned on his heel and marched out of the room.

Elizabeth didn't move. She had never felt more helpless in her life.

"Sarah—" Calvin began, then stopped. "I don't know what's happening here. I mean, this doesn't make sense. But let's go home, and in the morning—"

"What home?" Elizabeth snapped. "I don't have a home."

"Okay, fine. I can take you to Rhonda's—"

"I don't know any Rhondas."

"Okay, a hotel then. Though I don't know what we'll find at this time of night." He watched her silently, then said, "Now, this is just a suggestion—don't be offended. I think you should come back to my house for the night. *You* don't remember, but Sarah considered it home. I promise that we'll take care of you. And in the morning we'll come see this quack Dr. Waite."

Elizabeth looked up at him and noticed for the first time that his eyes were blue. She wanted to trust him. Under the circumstances, what other choice did she have?

"All right," she said. "Thank you."

Calvin smiled. "I'm just so happy that you came back to me."

They gathered Sarah's things and left.

The sun was rising as Elizabeth and Calvin drove back to Calvin's house. In the dim light of dawn, Elizabeth had a better chance to look at the town. It was both familiar and unfamiliar, like a picture that someone had tampered with—correct in most respects, but altered just enough to seem false. Buildings were in the wrong places, names changed, even one-way streets were reversed. The gas station where she and Jeff once stopped to put air in their bicycle tires was now a fast-food restaurant. The abandoned bowling alley that was due for demolition was a pristine multi-screen movie theater complex. How was it possible?

"This *is* Fawlt Line, isn't it?" Elizabeth asked after they passed what should have been the Fawlt Line Diner but was now called "Hank's."

"You remember Fawlt Line? Hey, we're making progress!" Calvin said.

"Fawlt Line is the name of *my* town, too," Elizabeth replied.

Calvin sighed.

Elizabeth sighed too, as she watched the morning sun splash orange on a town she recognized but didn't know.

They pulled up the driveway to Calvin's house and, as they approached the front porch, Elizabeth felt the same disjointed sense of reality. The house was Victorian like her own, but parts of it had shifted around. The chimney that should have thrust up from the living room on the left side was now sticking out of some other room on the right. Windows were in odd places. The color was a different shade of gray. Even the stained-glass window above the front door had changed from an elaborate rose to a sun shining behind a hill.

Calvin's parents, Ted and Barbara Collins, were waiting for them at the kitchen table, dressed in bathrobes and looking like unmade beds.

"Well?" Mrs. Collins asked as she sipped her coffee.

Elizabeth observed that the woman wouldn't look at her. *She doesn't like me*, Elizabeth knew instinctively. *She doesn't care how I am. Or she doesn't care how* Sarah *is.* "Which one of us don't you like?" Elizabeth wanted to ask.

"We'll get some sleep and then take her back to see another doctor," Calvin answered.

"I don't like this," Mr. Collins croaked in a scratchy morning voice. "So help me, if this is another one of her stunts. . . ."

Her stunts? He spoke as if Elizabeth—or Sarah—wasn't in the same room.

"We'll talk later," Calvin snapped and left the kitchen.

"I'm so sorry," Elizabeth said. "I wish I knew what was happening here. I wish I—" Their looks of surprise stopped her from finishing.

"She's learned how to apologize," Mrs. Collins said with a snort.

"Now there's a miracle," Mr. Collins replied.

Calvin called from the other room, "This way, Sarah—er, Elizabeth!"

Elizabeth walked to the stairs and followed Calvin up to her room. It felt like a lifetime since she had come out of the tub and into this strange dream.

In Sarah's room, Calvin gestured like a bellboy to a new guest in a hotel. "The bathroom is there and your bed's there and . . . and . . . maybe you'll remember more after you've had some sleep."

"Maybe I will," Elizabeth said, but she didn't believe it.

Calvin took a step forward, reaching for her hand. Elizabeth stepped back, nearly tripping over the lamp she had broken earlier.

"I'll clean that up later," he said.

"I'll do it," Elizabeth said automatically.

For a moment he looked puzzled. "Something *is* different," he said. "Before last night you never would've offered to do that."

"You mean, clean up after myself?"

"Yeah."

What kind of girl is this Sarah? Elizabeth wondered, then shrugged. "It's my mess. I'll clean it up."

"Okay." Calvin moved to the doorway and turned with his hand on the knob. "I'll wake you in a few hours."

"Thank you," Elizabeth said gently. She was truly grateful now. What would she have done if he hadn't been so nice to her?

He smiled and pulled the door closed.

The familiarity of the bathroom gave her the creeps. She was tempted to take another bath in the hope that it would somehow take her back to her own home—like Dorothy tapping her red shoes in *The Wizard of Oz.*

She leaned over the sink and looked at her puffy, tired face in the mirror. Had she lost her mind? Was she some kind of amnesiac?

She shook her head. Amnesiacs were people who *lost* their memories. She'd never heard of an amnesiac who traded one set of memories for another. If she really were Sarah, then where in the world did all of Elizabeth's memories come from? She remembered her home. She remembered the events of her life. Her fifth birthday when she sneaked in and ate half the icing off the cake before her party began. The day her mother stumbled all over her words as she tried to explain the facts of life. The Saturday when she was ten and her dad took her horseback riding for the first and last time (she goaded the horse so badly that it went wild, scaring the life out of her). And all too clearly she remembered that last fight with her mom and dad, and her conversation with Jeff at the diner. She was planning to run away from home.

How could she remember such details if it were only her mind playing tricks?

Returning to her room, she was surprised to find Calvin laying out fresh clothes on the bed. He spun around apologetically. "Sorry—I thought maybe you wouldn't remember where your clothes were."

"I probably wouldn't have."

"I know it's a stupid thing to think about, but—" Calvin blushed. "It occurred to me that you don't have your purse. Do you know where it is?"

"My purse? No, I don't know where it is." Elizabeth was perplexed. If she couldn't remember her own name, why would she remember where her purse was?

"Like I said, it's a stupid thing to think about." He backed toward the door. "It really is good to have you home again."

Again?

CHAPTER 10

Sheriff Hounslow led Jeff into a stark, windowless interrogation room in the Fawlt Line Police Station. It had all the charm of a medieval torture chamber and the looks to match. The building itself was a gray granite fortress modeled after an ancient English castle. The inside was marginally more modern. At least they had tried to paint the granite an industrial green.

Jeff looked at the scarred wooden table that could have served as a rack. Four metal folding chairs surrounded it like torturer's assistants.

"You want anything to drink?" Hounslow asked.

Jeff said thanks, but no, and the sheriff walked out. Jeff paced for a moment, then sat down. The fluorescent light flickered above him. That—plus the industrial green walls—made him feel seasick. Or maybe he was just nervous. He'd never been questioned by the police before.

What weighed on his mind even more, though, was Elizabeth. He wracked his brain for possible explanations, but nothing fit. She must have run away on her own. What other explanation was there?

No. Jeff didn't buy it. She wouldn't run away without letting someone know, without someone's help. Sure, she could be stubborn and independent, but not so much that she'd run away alone. Something was definitely wrong.

The door opened, and Alan and Jane Forde were escorted in by Sheriff Hounslow. "Please sit down," the sheriff said, gesturing to the dented, brown folding chairs.

Mr. Forde glanced around the room, then at Jeff. He managed a faint smile. Jeff smiled back. Mrs. Forde looked at him silently through puffy eyes. Hers was the face of every dark thought and every worry any of them could have about Elizabeth's whereabouts. Jeff's heart took a downward turn.

Mr. Forde pulled out a chair for his wife to sit on. She grabbed the table as if the effort would send her to the floor instead. Struck by an unaccountable feeling of responsibility, Jeff looked away at one of the windowless walls and wished his uncle were present. But Malcolm was well on his way to Washington, Jeff knew. He wondered if the police had called Mrs. Packer.

"Coffee for anyone?" Sheriff Hounslow asked politely.

They all shook their heads no.

The sheriff waited until all eyes were on him. "I'm sorry, Alan—Jane. I know how difficult this is for you," he said. "Maybe Jeff will be so kind as to tell us everything he knows about Elizabeth. Maybe he'll start by telling us where she is right now."

Surprised at the sheriff's insinuation, Jeff looked up at him, then across the table at Mr. and Mrs. Forde. "I don't know where she is," Jeff said. "Honest. If I did, I'd tell you."

"I'd like to believe you, Jeff," the sheriff said. "But I know how close you two were and . . . well, you'd do anything for Elizabeth, wouldn't you?"

"Almost anything."

"Like keep a secret? Y'know . . . if she asked you not to tell anyone where she was, then you might not tell, right?"

Jeff shook his head. "This is too serious. I'd tell."

Hounslow leaned forward. "Okay, then, Jeff. Go ahead and explain to Mr. and Mrs. Forde what you were doing at the Old Sawmill."

"I was waiting for Elizabeth to meet me," Jeff admitted.

In an identical movement, Mr. and Mrs. Forde turned to face Jeff. "Why?" Mr. Forde asked.

"She wanted to run away from home—the two of us, I mean," Jeff said reluctantly. Then he blurted defensively, "But I wasn't going to do it. I was going to talk her out of it."

"Why would she want to run away from home?" Mrs. Forde whispered.

Jeff shrugged. "You know how Elizabeth is. She got mad and decided to leave."

"Whom was she mad at?" Mr. Forde asked.

Jeff didn't want to answer the question. He didn't want to get into family squabbles at a time like this. He looked helplessly at the sheriff, hoping he'd intervene, but Hounslow merely cocked an eyebrow in response.

"At you two," Jeff finally said.

Mrs. Forde opened her mouth to react, but Mr. Forde put his hand on her arm and nodded, as if no further explanation were needed. "What do we do now, Sheriff?" he asked.

Hounslow sat up straight. "If we're willing to believe that Jeff doesn't know where she is—"

"Jeff wouldn't lie," Mr. Forde said simply. "Let's get on with whatever we have to do."

The sheriff scratched his cheek. "Then maybe you should tell me why Elizabeth was mad at you."

Mr. Forde stared at Hounslow for a moment. It was hard to tell if the sheriff was asking a routine question or implying more. Mr. Forde cleared his throat. "Unless Jeff can say otherwise, I believe that I'm an endless source of embarrassment to my daughter."

All eyes fell on Jeff, as if he might disagree. Instead he blushed.

Mr. Forde went on, "I can't believe she would really run away, though. I can't be so unbearable that she'd—" He fell silent and slumped in his chair a little.

"Shouldn't we be out looking for her?" Mrs. Forde asked in a strained voice.

Sheriff Hounslow sighed. "Maybe she's gone off on her own for a while. It happens with teenage girls."

"No," Mrs. Forde said adamantly. "No one has heard from her—something is *wrong!*"

Hounslow stood up. "We can do some checking around, but technically I can't issue a missing person's report for at least twenty-four hours. I suggest you go home so you'll be there when she cools down and comes back."

Mr. Forde looked as if he might argue. Then, apparently changing his mind, he stood. After helping Mrs. Forde out of her chair, he said to Jeff, "If you hear from her, you'll let us know?"

"Yes, sir," Jeff replied.

Mr. and Mrs. Forde slowly walked out of the room. "God help us," Mrs. Forde whispered as they disappeared around the corner.

"Are you sure there isn't anything else you want to tell me?" the sheriff asked.

"No."

"You had some kind of fight at the diner, didn't you?"

Jeff bristled. "We didn't have a *fight*. Elizabeth and I don't fight. She was mad at her parents, I told you. What are you trying to say?"

Sheriff Hounslow shrugged. "I'm not 'trying to say' anything. I'm just asking questions. Come on, I'll have one of the boys take you home. Maybe your Uncle Malcolm has some suggestions. He seems to know everything there is to know about everything." The hint of sarcasm was hard to miss.

"Uncle Malcolm's out of town," Jeff said coldly.

"Too bad," the sheriff said. "I'll bet he could impress us all and find Elizabeth in no time."

Mrs. Packer was waiting for Jeff when he walked through the front door. Her disheveled hair and untidy robe told him that she'd been roused suddenly from her bed. Her stern face was framed by strands of white hair that had sprung loose from their pins. She wasn't happy.

"Malcolm called from his hotel room in Washington," she said as if the call's being long-distance made it all the more inconvenient. "He wanted to know how your evening went with Elizabeth. I told him that she's missing."

"How did you know—?"

"The police came here to see if you knew where she was."

"Oh, I'm sorry," Jeff said.

"So you should be," she said. "Things like this wouldn't happen if you kids weren't allowed to run loose at all hours of the evening—"

44

"Did Uncle Malcolm leave a message?" Jeff asked.

Mrs. Packer frowned at losing her chance to lecture him. "He said he's sorry and that he'll pray for her—and you."

"Is that all?" His expression of disappointment was unmistakable. He had hoped Uncle Malcolm would jump on the first plane home. Sarcastic or not, Sheriff Hounslow was right. Uncle Malcolm *could* find Elizabeth. "Is that all he said?"

"Is that all?!?" Mrs. Packer said indignantly as she gathered up the bottom of her robe and marched up the stairs. "As a matter of fact, it's more than enough!"

But it wasn't enough for Jeff. He slipped out the front door and into the cool night to find Elizabeth.

CHAPTER 11

The *Fawlt Line Daily Gazette* ran the story about Elizabeth's disappearance. It even mentioned that she had disappeared from a locked bathroom in a tub full of water. The entire town talked about it in shops and restaurants; the consensus was that Elizabeth had taken off for a new life somewhere, probably in the "big city." Even Helen, the supposedly psychic telephone operator, was quoted as saying she had a feeling that Elizabeth was long gone.

Jeff resented the gossip and speculation. Elizabeth was gone, but he was certain she hadn't run away. She was in trouble. Maybe kidnapped. Maybe . . .

Jeff shuddered to think about it.

Searchers combed the woods, empty buildings, shacks, old wells—anywhere she might have accidentally gotten herself trapped . . . or hidden on purpose. Every neighborhood, block, lone street or alleyway, country lane and abandoned tract of land was explored. Jeff investigated on his own, checking places that he and Elizabeth had been, even places they'd only talked about. Anywhere Jeff could think of, he searched.

At eleven o'clock that morning, the town reacted to a rumor that Elizabeth was seen in the company of an older dark-haired man with a tattoo on his forearm at the Park & Dine Truck Stop way out on Route 40. The police found the man and his companion at the truck stop, all right—only "Elizabeth" was a sixty-three-year-old woman in a black wig.

Mr. and Mrs. Forde offered a reward to anyone who could provide information. Jeff ached for them. He could imagine how terrible they felt, losing their daughter and suspecting that it was somehow their fault. He wished he could say something to comfort them, but he wasn't very good at talking to adults. With the exception of Uncle Malcolm, they made him uneasy. Especially Sheriff Hounslow.

The sheriff had stopped by first thing that morning to ask Jeff more questions. Jeff was sick of repeating his story. What was Sheriff Hounslow doing, trying to trick him into some kind of confession?

As the day went on, Jeff had to wonder: was it his imagination, or was he seeing the sheriff at unexpected times in unexpected places? Police cars showed up as he rounded a street corner in his Volkswagen or stepped out of a shop. Jeff wasn't paranoid enough to believe they were following him. But maybe they were. Maybe they thought he knew where Elizabeth was and hoped to catch him meeting her.

The issue was put to rest late in the afternoon when Jeff arrived at home. As he put the key into the door lock, someone tapped on his shoulder.

"Hi, Jeff," Sheriff Hounslow said. "Okay if we talk for a couple of minutes?"

"I guess so," Jeff said, but he didn't invite the sheriff into the house. They remained on the porch.

"I'd like you to tell me again about your last conversation with Elizabeth and why you were waiting for her at the Old Sawmill."

Jeff sighed impatiently. "How many times do I have to tell you?"

"As many times as it takes, I guess," the sheriff said pleasantly.

"Why? Do you suspect me of something? Do you think you'll catch me in a lie? *What do you really want to know?*"

Sheriff Hounslow hitched his thumbs in his belt and leaned against the doorpost. "Put yourself in my position, Jeff. Besides her parents, you're the last person who talked to Elizabeth. And according to witnesses, you had an argument—"

"We *didn't* have an argument!"

"A heated discussion then—I don't care what you call it. All I know is that the customers there saw what they saw. Then her parents report her as missing, we learn that she was supposed to meet you at the Old Sawmill and, lo and behold, we find you waiting for her there. But there's no sign of Elizabeth—anywhere. What are my options?"

Jeff didn't answer. He knew the sheriff would tell him anyway.

"My options are that Elizabeth really did run away on her own. But you and her parents say she wouldn't do that. What am I supposed to think? She was kidnapped? There's no ransom note, no phone call. And nobody saw any strangers around town that day or evening, so I'm not inclined to think that she's in the clutches of some maniac.

"So it comes back to you. You're her best friend, and you were going to help her run away. So I'm thinking that maybe she's hiding somewhere, and you know where but you're not saying."

"That's not true—"

"Yeah, yeah, save your protest." Sheriff Hounslow stood up straight again. "But if I were a big-city detective, I might not be so trusting. I might think that you're not telling us the whole truth about your argument at the diner or why you were meeting Elizabeth at the Old Sawmill. I might even think that something worse happened between you."

So it was out. This was what the sheriff was after.

Jeff felt the heat rise through his entire body, flushing his cheeks and breaking a sweat on his brow. "You think I did something to her?"

"I'm just saying what I *might* think under certain circumstances, that's all."

Jeff's eyes burned. All day he had felt trapped between the hope that Elizabeth would suddenly turn up and the fear that she was gone for good. All day he had searched with a knot in the pit of his stomach, afraid that he might find her—but not safe or healthy. All day he had hoped for the best but expected the worst. That's what he had learned to do after his parents died; it was the only way to cope with life. Expect the unexpected. But he *never* expected to be a suspect himself in Elizabeth's disappearance. He clenched his teeth as the anger rushed to his tongue. He tried to hold it back.

"Something you want to say to me, Jeff?" Sheriff Hounslow asked.

Jeff opened his mouth to rail against his accuser. Suddenly the front door opened. Jeff and the sheriff both turned.

Uncle Malcolm smiled at his nephew. "Hello, Jeff."

"When did you get home?"

"About an hour ago," he said, then turned a hard look toward the sheriff. "If you're going to persist in questioning my ward, let's go down to your office and I'll make sure a lawyer is present."

Hounslow coughed nervously and said, "It's not necessary, Malcolm. We were just having a friendly chat."

"Uh huh," Malcolm said. "Well, if you'll excuse us, Jeff and I need to have a friendly chat too."

Hounslow nodded to Malcolm, shot a fiery glance at Jeff, and strode off the porch and down the walk.

Relieved, Jeff blew out his cheeks and wiped his forehead. "Uncle Malcolm—"

"I know." Malcolm smiled. "He's a little too diligent with his job."

"He thinks *I* did something to Elizabeth!"

Malcolm put his hand on Jeff's arm. "Don't let it bother you. But if it's not too much trouble, I want you to come in and tell me everything that happened after I left."

Jeff sighed. *Here we go again.*

Malcolm's eyes twinkled. "I have a theory."

CHAPTER 12

If there had been any doubt before, there wasn't now. Dr. Kenneth Waite, a dark-haired man with piercing blue eyes and a staff psychiatrist badge on his white coat, was certain.

Elizabeth had amnesia.

But unlike the kind of amnesia she knew from watching television—where the hero gets conked on the head and forgets who he is until someone conks him on the head again—Elizabeth had hysterical amnesia.

He leaned back in his chair and threaded his fingers together. "It's a stress-induced amnesia brought on by an unknown mental trauma."

"What kind of trauma?" Calvin asked from the chair next to Elizabeth's.

Dr. Waite nodded as if he appreciated the intelligence of Calvin's question. "We've seen it in cases of abuse or rape, where the victim goes into deep denial not only about the event itself, but about his or her entire life. Other cases have included the sudden death of a loved one—"

"Your parents!" Calvin blurted to Elizabeth. "Maybe it's a delayed reaction."

Elizabeth cringed.

"Maybe," Dr. Waite allowed. "Trauma comes in many forms."

After hours of sitting on cold hospital carts, enduring endless questions, having her head scanned by bizarre-looking machines, and struggling to keep her sanity in this nightmare, she had had enough. "You want trauma? I'll give you one: how about a girl takes a bath, and when she gets out of the tub finds herself in a completely different world where everyone calls her by someone else's name? That's a trauma for you."

Dr. Waite smiled indulgently from across his large oak desk. "Sarah—"

"Elizabeth," she corrected him.

"The sooner you accept this situation, the sooner we can begin the healing process."

"If you want to heal me, then figure out how to get me home!" Elizabeth shouted, rising to her feet.

Calvin shifted in his seat nervously. "What about that? I mean, you say she's got amnesia, but she remembers all kinds of things. But they're things that she never did."

"I did, too!" she said, falling back in her chair, arms folded.

Dr. Waite leaned forward. "In certain types of trauma resulting in this type of amnesia, it's not uncommon for the patient to create an alternative memory—or, shall we say, *reality*—that seems happier or more preferable to the reality that he or she is in. We call that *paramnesia*, where dreams or fantasies become the reality."

Elizabeth frowned. "You're making this up as you go along, aren't you?"

"So what do we do?" Calvin asked.

"I think we should admit her to the hospital for observation," Dr. Waite said. "Perhaps try a session with sodium amobarbital."

"Uh-uh." Elizabeth shook her head. "No hospital, and definitely no drugs."

Calvin turned to her. "Just for a couple of days."

"He wants to drug me up and put me in the loony ward," Elizabeth said, still shaking her head.

"Now, now," Dr. Waite protested. "There are merely other patients there with non-aggressive psychological conditions."

"No. I won't do it."

Dr. Waite tapped the leather blotter on his desk. "Legally, we don't need your permission, Sarah. Calvin's parents have already signed the forms. But I'd rather have you agree."

Elizabeth frowned stubbornly.

"I thought you wanted to go home," Dr. Waite said.

"I do."

"Then this may be the way to get there."

"What're you talking about?"

"If you are Elizabeth, and this is as you say some kind of

nightmare, then we may be able to wake you out of it. For all you know, I am really a doctor from *your* reality trying to reach you through your consciousness. The same is true if you are Sarah, somehow lost in a dream called Elizabeth. Either way, we want to bring the *real* person back to where she belongs. And time spent here will help us to do that."

Elizabeth eyed him skeptically. It made sense in a strange, gibberish sort of way. "But you're not going to spend all your time trying to convince me that I'm Sarah, right?"

Dr. Waite shook his head slowly. "We won't try to convince you of anything. We'll let Elizabeth and Sarah take care of that."

"I get a room of my own?" Elizabeth asked as Dr. Waite got her settled in a plain white cell off the psychiatric wing. Calvin had gone home to get her clothes, toothbrush, and toiletries. "I thought these loony-bin rooms were always shared."

"Your boyfriend says his family will spare no expense for you," Dr. Waite replied.

Elizabeth remembered the cold, uncaring expressions on Calvin's parents' faces and couldn't imagine that they would give her a dime, let alone an expensive room in a hospital.

"I must warn you," Dr. Waite said from the doorway, "that people will call you Sarah. It's the only name they know. Your—er, *her* friends will come to visit. You need to be understanding if they don't acknowledge you as Elizabeth."

Elizabeth shrugged. "I'll cope."

"Good. Let me know if you need anything." He strolled into the hall, looking first in both directions as if checking traffic at a pedestrian crossing.

Elizabeth sat on the edge of the pristine bed and looked around at the clinically correct room with its assembled metal and Formica furniture on wheels. *There's no place like home*, she thought again, mentally tapping red shoes.

She had promised herself when she woke up that morning to play it tough. No crying, complaining, or whining. She'd be a rock, no matter what happened. That was the way to be. Tough as nails.

Deep inside she figured she might be able to will herself out of this dream.

And it was a dream. She knew that now. Dr. Waite himself had used the phrase. It was a dream and, if she were strong enough and could look it in the eyes long enough, she would wake herself up. She must simply hold on to what she knew to be true. *I am Elizabeth. Elizabeth. Elizabeth.*

"Sarah?"

Elizabeth looked up and suddenly realized that she wasn't sitting on the edge of the bed, but was lying on her side, her arms folded, her legs pulled up to her chest.

A pretty girl with enviable dimples and short brown hair stood in the doorway. She was wearing a loose, striped, pullover sweater, jeans, and white tennis shoes. She smiled, but her large eyes betrayed a certain amount of discomfort. "Hi ya," she said.

Elizabeth slid off the bed but stood next to it. For the moment, it was her life raft. "Are you a nurse?"

The pretty girl looked crestfallen for a moment, but recovered quickly. "No. Don't you remember me?"

"Sorry," Elizabeth said. "I don't remember anything that people think I should remember."

"Huh?"

Elizabeth waved to a chair. "I guess you can sit down if you know me. Maybe you can tell me something about myself."

The pretty girl moved to the chair but stopped midway. She was closer to Elizabeth now and spoke in a low whisper. "You really don't remember me? I mean, this isn't one of your stunts, is it?"

One of your stunts. One of her stunts. So it wasn't just Calvin's parents who had a low opinion of this Sarah's behavior.

"I don't know what you're talking about," Elizabeth said.

The pretty girl resumed her walk to the chair and sat down. "It's okay. I was just checking. I heard what happened and . . . well, I didn't know what to believe."

"I don't want to be rude," Elizabeth said, "but . . . who are you?"

"Rhonda."

For a second, Elizabeth wished the name would trigger her memory. But the wish immediately scared her and she retracted it. How could she wish for a memory as Sarah that she knew couldn't be true for Elizabeth? This Rhonda Whoeversheis was a stranger. *Elizabeth* didn't know her.

"Okay, Rhonda. Please don't be offended when I say that I don't know who you are. Should I?"

The pretty girl called Rhonda chuckled. "Seriously?"

"Seriously."

Rhonda smiled, her dimples deeply angelic. "Yeah, you know me. I'm your best friend."

The phrase *best friend* caught Elizabeth off guard, unexpectedly bringing to mind the best friends that she had had in her life. Karen Adams. Michelle Warburg. Melissa Morgan.

But one best friend, in particular, filled her thoughts. Jeff. Jeff, who was supposed to meet her at the Old Sawmill. Jeff, whom she could count on and confide in and complain to, whom she considered her best friend above and beyond the call of best-friend duty. Jeff. Would she ever see him again?

With the image of his face, the rock shattered, the supposedly tough nails bent and broke. Elizabeth found herself weeping in the arms of this *other* best friend whom she had only just met.

CHAPTER

"I had a dream last night that all the buttons came off my dress. I rushed for my sewing kit, and when I found it, I realized that my fingers were gone. I had two stumps instead of hands. I was upset because I couldn't sew the buttons back on my dress. I woke up screaming." The silver-haired woman dropped her head onto her chest as if reliving the dream had drained her of all her energy.

Elizabeth shifted nervously in an uncomfortable wooden chair, one of a half-dozen chairs gathered in a semicircle for Dr. Waite's afternoon therapy group.

Another woman in her early thirties detailed her adventures as a silent movie screen actress in a previous life. She also announced that, in a life before that, she was Genghis Khan's wife.

A man with jet-black, greased-back hair and a chiseled face told the group how he saw his dead wife on the bus yesterday afternoon. Apparently he'd forgotten that he hadn't been out of the hospital for weeks.

An old man with kind eyes and thin lines of white hair pasted across a spotted scalp remembered the day a bomb killed his family during the London Blitz. Dr. Waite smiled indulgently and reminded the man that he had never been out of the country, let alone in London during World War II. "Oh," the man said, accepting the correction indifferently. "My mistake."

All Elizabeth could think, now that she had heard four different stories like this, was that she was definitely in the wrong place. She didn't belong here with this group of mixed nuts. What did her particular nightmare have to do with the neurotic dreams and strange compulsions of these poor mentally disturbed people? She was not mentally disturbed. Or was she? Suddenly she realized that to Dr. Waite, Calvin, and everyone else, her denial of being Sarah—her insistence that she had another life as someone called Elizabeth—must sound exactly like these testimonies sounded to her. *Insane.*

She brooded on that thought as a hospital maintenance worker in white overalls entered. He glanced apologetically at Dr. Waite and the group, but Elizabeth was the only one who took any notice. He was an older man, maybe sixty, his dark hair adorned by patches of white at the temples. The white patches suggested an age his face didn't seem to show. It struck Elizabeth instantly: *he looks like a young man trapped in an old man's body.* The worker moved quickly to a table at the far end of the room and busied himself stacking a tray of dirty coffee cups.

Dr. Waite cleared his throat, and Elizabeth was aware that all eyes were on her. "We're waiting to hear from you," he said softly.

"What do you want me to say?"

"Why not start with your name?" he answered. It was a challenge.

She sat up straight in her uncomfortable wooden chair. "My name is Elizabeth, but everyone seems to think I'm someone else named Sarah." She faltered for a moment until Dr. Waite encouraged her to tell the group everything she could. Reluctantly, she did—beginning with her life with her dad and mom in Fawlt Line, continuing with the bath, and ending at the point where Calvin brought her to the hospital. The group nodded at her with great understanding. The silent-movie-star-and-wife-of-Genghis-Khan dabbed a tissue at her eyes.

Elizabeth felt like crying too. The last thing she wanted was the affirmation of these wackos.

Dr. Waite announced to the group that their purpose was to help synthesize Elizabeth and Sarah into one whole and healthy person. He never used the term "hysterical amnesia," but it hung over his carefully chosen words.

At least he kept his promise, Elizabeth thought. *He isn't trying to convert me into believing I'm Sarah.* But she was worn down now. She felt discouraged, unsure of herself.

Cups rattled as the hospital maintenance man disappeared out the door with his tray. *Okay, let's be honest for a minute,* she thought. What if she stepped outside of herself and looked realistically at her situation, just for a minute? There she was, a young girl whom everyone knew as Sarah. There were Calvin and his parents, her "best friend" Rhonda, and no doubt scores of others with individual memories of her as Sarah. They could each tell stories about her, present an entire history of her life that was completely flawless in its truthfulness. To the entire world, she was Sarah. But she alone insisted that she was Elizabeth. She alone had memories of her mother and father, Jeff, her Fawlt Line. . . .

The therapy group ended, and the worm of doubt followed Elizabeth back to her room. She was startled to find several bouquets of flowers, all accompanied by expressions of love from Calvin. And he had brought in framed photographs—of her alone, her with him, even one of her with Rhonda.

She was touched but not comforted. Which *her* was she looking at? Was it Elizabeth in those photos or Sarah?

Elizabeth stared at a picture of herself—of Sarah—with Calvin. In it her hair was a different style, shorter. She looked younger. Calvin looked younger, too, and less beefy. But they looked very happy.

"Rhonda took that right after you moved in with my family," Calvin said from over her shoulder. Elizabeth didn't move, but locked her eyes on the photo.

"I'm sorry. I don't remember."

"That's okay," he said. "You will. And even if you don't, I believe we can start all over again. Maybe it's even better this way. A second chance to do everything right. To fix the things that went wrong." He put his hands on her shoulders. "I love you, whoever you are. I just want you to know that."

Elizabeth turned away. Not to the flowers or photos, but to the window, which looked out onto a parking lot filled with cars that sparkled like jewels in the afternoon sun.

"It's too much to take in," Calvin said. "I know. Forget I said anything. How about business? Can we talk about business?"

"Business?"

"Nobody knows where your purse is."

Elizabeth was confused. "My purse?"

"It's gone. Maybe you took it out with you and left it somewhere. Who knows? We can't find it. But we need to make arrange-
ments to get you some new identification. Y'know, driver's permit,
student ID, and all that."

The significance was lost on her. "Sure. Go ahead."

He scratched his chin. "So . . . I should just have them replaced."

Elizabeth turned to face him again. "Yes," she said, puzzlement
in her voice.

"The identification will be in your name . . . I mean, Sarah's
name. You'll be Sarah."

Now she understood. The question of the day.

Are you Elizabeth or Sarah? Just who exactly are you?

The evidence of many witnesses . . . the proof . . . her own reason all told her that she must be Sarah. Whatever happened in the
tub—whatever she thought she remembered as Elizabeth—was
completely outweighed by the facts.

Elizabeth looked at Calvin. He had been so nice to her—kind,
caring, even charming. She clenched and unclenched her fists. She
thought about being held by Rhonda as she cried her eyes out earlier. She thought of the reality of this room and the smell of the flowers and the view from the window. It was real. All of her senses said
that it was. *So what are those other memories? What are those scenes and
people and feelings from some other place?* The evidence was stacked
up, layer upon layer, on her will and resolve. Even her own senses
testified against her.

How could she withstand it and *not* go crazy?

Are you Elizabeth or Sarah?

Why not play along? See what happens?

Are you Elizabeth or Sarah?

At least there would be peace in a decision. She wouldn't be at
war with a truth that seemed obvious to everyone but her.

Are you Elizabeth or Sarah?

"You win," she said to Calvin, but really to the world. "I'm
Sarah."

CHAPTER 14

In his uncle's study Jeff repeated exactly what had happened, beginning with his trip to the Old Sawmill to wait for Elizabeth, while Uncle Malcolm listened quietly. When he finished his tale, he sank back into the solace of the thick-cushioned chair.

Mrs. Packer entered with a tray bearing a pot of hot tea. Jeff declined it, but Uncle Malcolm, with a thoughtful expression, poured milk into the extremely large mug that served as his tea cup. Jeff relaxed. Somehow the very ordinary activity of having tea in his uncle's study gave him a sense of security . . . a refuge from the distress of the past day.

"You didn't mention one little item that the newspaper reported," Uncle Malcolm said to Jeff.

"What's that?"

"The locked bathroom door," Uncle Malcolm answered, sipping his tea. "That's the thing that gets my attention. I know the Fordes' house—at least its age. I assume the rooms still have doors that lock with a key."

Jeff had to think about it for a moment, then he nodded. "Yeah, they do."

"If Alan Forde is telling the truth, and I'm inclined to believe he is, then how could the door be locked from the inside without Elizabeth being in there?"

Jeff sat up. "I hadn't thought about that."

Uncle Malcolm rested his chin on his hand. With his book-shelves behind him, he looked as though he were posing for a family portrait. "Why would Elizabeth go to all the trouble of filling the tub and somehow locking the door from the inside in order to run away? Also, according to the newspaper, Alan Forde said that none of her clothes were missing. What do you make of that?"

Jeff shook his head. "I don't know. What do *you* make of it? You said you have a theory."

"I have a theory, all right," he chuckled. "But I don't expect anyone to believe it—not even you."

"Try me," Jeff offered.

Uncle Malcolm got out of his chair and paced with his head lifted up and his hands clasped behind his back. "Brace yourself, Jeff. You're going to need every ounce of imagination you can muster."

"Okay," Jeff said, not sure what was coming.

"For years I've been fascinated with various forms of paranormal and psychic phenomena. Not fortunetellers and freaks," he qualified with a raised finger, "but unexplainable experiences. History is filled with them."

"What's this have to do with Elizabeth?"

Uncle Malcolm smiled. "I've been exploring the possibility of a relationship between certain states of mind and the very sudden, unexplainable disappearances of people."

"You're kidding," Jeff said. "Are you going to tell me you think Elizabeth was kidnapped by aliens or something?"

"Nope."

"Good."

"But I could give you an entire history lesson about missing persons. Not only individuals but entire villages." Uncle Malcolm paced silently for a moment. "I've never told anyone this, but I've put a lot of pieces together and discovered that Fawlt Line has its own strange history. There's a reason this town is so quirky, and I have a theory about that, too. But for now I'll stick to disappearances. Like Charles Richards. Ever heard of him?"

Jeff hadn't.

"Langham Richards was a big investor in tobacco around here and made a lot of money. To his chagrin, his son Charles opted for a modest life as a farmer rather than becoming a wealthy merchant. That was interrupted by the Korean War. He was twenty-two years old and was drafted. In 1954 Charles came back from the service, built a house for himself, his wife, and two kids on a small farm just outside of Fawlt Line, and settled down to a life as a young gentleman farmer."

Jeff shifted in his chair, and Uncle Malcolm sensed he was losing his audience's interest.

"Bear with me," he continued. "One morning the two kids, Susan and Donald, were playing next to the sidewalk leading from the house to the front gate. Charles and his wife, Julia, stepped out of the front door. Charles had some errands to take care of at the bank in Fawlt Line. He kissed his wife good-bye and walked down the steps toward the kids. Julia stayed at the door, watching. Charles patted his kids on their heads as he walked past. They giggled and waved. He reached the front gate, pausing as a car came up the road toward the house. It was driven by Dr. Hezekiah Beckett, the local veterinarian, who was dropping by to check on one of Charles's horses that had been sick. With him was a young boy who was helping the doctor that summer.

"Charles waved at the doctor and paused to check the time on his wristwatch. He then turned as if he were going to walk toward the approaching car to speak to Dr. Beckett. He took three steps and, in full view of his wife, his children, Dr. Beckett, and the boy, *he disappeared*.

"His wife screamed. The children stood frozen. Dr. Beckett stopped the car, leapt out, and raced to the spot. A moment later Julia, the children, and the boy joined him. The five of them looked at the ground. They saw only the fence and the grass. No bushes, no trees to hide behind, no holes to fall into—nothing to give them any hint as to what had happened to Charles."

Jeff's wide eyes didn't move or blink.

Uncle Malcolm went on, "Dr. Beckett and Julia Richards searched everywhere. At least, they searched until Julia collapsed, hysterical. Dr. Beckett got help from the townspeople. Scores of folk arrived and searched every inch of Charles's land. Some even began to dig up the ground where Charles had disappeared, in the belief that he'd fallen into a sinkhole or underground cavern and was even then trapped below. But it was solid ground. Charles was gone. He had disappeared in full view of five people."

Jeff swallowed hard. "That's not the end of it. Please tell me that's not the end."

"It's not," Uncle Malcolm said. "Weeks went by, and the investigation faded for lack of any clues. Julia, Dr. Beckett, the kids, the young boy, all testified again and again that they saw the exact same thing. There was no explanation for it.

"Julia was bedridden for months, lost in the hope that her husband would return. They never had a funeral or a memorial service. Eventually, a year later, they sold the farm and moved away."

Jeff jumped out of his chair. "That's it? That's the end of the story? What are you trying to do to me, Uncle Malcolm? You made that up!"

"No, Jeff. It's fully documented. Not only do I have the written testimonies of everyone who was there, but I managed to get tape recordings of the witnesses. Do you want to hear them?"

"No!" Jeff shouted. "You hear stories like this all the time. We don't know those people. Maybe they were up to something. Maybe they were in cahoots to get Richards' money!"

"Calm down," Uncle Malcolm said. "I can assure you that they were not."

"Yeah? How do you know? How can anyone know?"

"Because I was the young boy in the car. I worked with Dr. Beckett that summer. I saw it with my own eyes."

Jeff stopped dead in his tracks to look at his uncle. Finally he said, "I don't get it. What's your point?"

"My point is that there are a lot of things in heaven and on earth that are beyond our comprehension. If you and the Fordes are telling the truth about Elizabeth's disappearance, then it's entirely possible that she went the way of Charles Richards. Don't you see? I've been waiting for years for an event like this to happen again. I knew it would. Particularly in Fawlt Line."

Jeff looked helplessly at Uncle Malcolm. There was no way to measure his love for the man, but this was too much to be believed. "That's your theory? You think that the people of Fawlt Line don't just disappear like normal people, but they disappear to . . . to where?"

"Ah! That's the other part of my theory," Malcolm proclaimed. "But I warn you: it'll be even harder for you to accept."

"Harder!"

Malcolm paused as if unsure about continuing. Then he took a deep breath and said, "I went to Washington to meet with a doctor friend of mine who has been studying phenomena like the story I just told you. Jeff, there are so many things we don't know or understand about time and space. But my friend's research gives strong indications that there's more going on than most of us are willing to grasp."

"Uh-oh. Here come the aliens," Jeff mocked.

"Not quite, but I want you to think about dreams for a minute."

"Dreams?"

Uncle Malcolm nodded. "I'm also interested in somnambulistic phenomena. That means dreams—the subconscious—and how they connect to the unexplainable, like the sudden disappearances. Now, what if there is a point of entry into another time or dimension of space . . . through a dream? What if things we often dismiss because we think they're just part of the imagination or a so-called dream are really a—how can I say it?—a glimpse into an alternative reality or time? What if, somehow, the brain crosses over and takes a peek at what's there? And *that's* what we're seeing?"

Blank now, Jeff could only look quizzically at his uncle.

Malcolm spread his hands. "And if the brain can do it, why not an entire body? Are you with me? That's what we're studying. We're suggesting that the mysterious disappearances of some of these people throughout history may mean that there's a *physical* point of entry between our world and whatever that other world is."

"But how?" Jeff asked. "How do you and your doctor friend think people physically jump from one place to the other?"

Uncle Malcolm looked embarrassed. "I don't know."

"But you think that if Elizabeth never turns up, it's possible that she sort of fell asleep in the bathtub and then just slipped over to another world somewhere?"

Uncle Malcolm smiled sheepishly.

Jeff wanted to believe him. He was desperate to believe that Elizabeth was safe and sound somewhere, even if that somewhere was somewhere impossible. But he couldn't believe. He didn't have that kind of faith. "Uncle Malcolm?"

"Yes, Jeff?"

"If I were you, I wouldn't mention your theory to anybody else."

CHAPTER 15

Elizabeth's day at the hospital was filled with daytime television programs she didn't recognize, but which were still awful; a casual chat with Dr. Waite who was pleased about her "decision" to work at being Sarah; and another round of therapy with the group, where the old man had amended his memories of being bombed out in the blitz to being a cook on a ship in the South Seas. Dr. Waite suggested that Elizabeth treat her memories like "another very realistic dream" and embrace Sarah's life in the here and now.

At dinner time, the nurse didn't come with her food. She was just about to buzz for it when Calvin arrived in a nice suit and tie, announcing that he had Dr. Waite's permission to take her out for the evening. Elizabeth was pleased, if only at the opportunity to get away from the hospital for a while, but realized that she didn't have any clothes to wear. Like a magician pulling a rabbit out of a hat, Calvin stepped into the hall and returned with a couple of outfits he'd picked from Sarah's closet.

While Calvin waited in the hall, Elizabeth quickly made her choice and slipped into a dress. It fit perfectly. Shaking off a gathering feeling of melancholy, she opened the door for Calvin, who rewarded her with a whistle and an approving smile.

They walked to Giovanni's, an Italian restaurant only two blocks from the hospital. "Doctor's orders," Calvin said as they sat at their table. "I couldn't take you too far—yet."

Elizabeth looked around at the cloth-covered tables, the formally dressed waiters, paintings, and more silverware than she knew how to use. She grinned to herself. *Jeff would be lost in a place like this.*

"So, what do we talk about?" Calvin asked after their fettucine and manicotti arrived. "Should I pretend you're a new arrival in town? Or maybe I should treat this like our very first date. Do you remember? You grilled me about my goals in life."

"Did I?"

"Yeah." He chuckled. "I felt like I was being interviewed. But that's the way you are. A no-nonsense kind of girl. You weren't about to hook up with a loser."

Elizabeth put down her fork. "You make me sound like a mercenary."

Calvin shrugged. "You're a girl who knows what she wants. Nothing wrong with that."

Elizabeth considered the phrase. Wasn't it really a nice way of saying that Sarah was self-serving? "Go on," she said.

"Let's see . . . you know, er, knew I'm a junior in high school, hoping to get a scholarship to the U, and I'm doing a student internship at the bank."

"You want to be a banker?" Elizabeth said in surprise. "Bankers are supposed to be wimpy little guys with glasses and starched collars. You won't qualify."

Calvin laughed. "Thank you. But I don't really plan to be a banker. I want to work in investments. I'm going to study business in college."

"Is that what you're really interested in?"

"I'm being practical. Trends and technology come and go, but we'll always need people who know about money." He pushed his fettucine around for a moment, then gave her a tender look. "You've encouraged me a lot. You helped me understand where my strengths are."

"Oh, I'm a saint." Elizabeth laughed.

"Saint Sarah."

"Patron Saint of the Forlorn and Forgotten," Elizabeth continued, then stopped. That wasn't so funny.

Calvin lifted his Coke to her. "Or Patron Saint of the Newly Remembered."

The moment was recovered, and she lifted her glass of water.

"To the future," he said softly.

She gazed at him, then sighed and put her glass down.

"Sorry," he said.

She shook her head. "You don't have to apologize. You've been very, very nice to me and . . . I'm so confused."

Calvin reached across the table and gently placed his hand on hers. "No pressure," he said. "I guess I'm just relieved to be here with you. We've had a hard time lately and—well, it's nice to have you back, even though you're not all the way back. If you know what I mean."

Elizabeth smiled noncommittally and turned her attention to the food on her plate. Calvin told her more about things they had done together. It created a picture for her of two very happy and obviously wealthy teens. She wondered where all the money came from, but she didn't inquire. Her parents had always said it was rude to ask about financial matters.

Hesitantly Elizabeth ventured back to their previous conversation. "Calvin, it sounds like we were having the time of our lives. So . . . why were we having problems?"

He hedged. "If you don't remember, why go into it? It's over now."

"But—"

"We can have a new beginning," he said brightly. "I don't want to be insensitive, but . . . in a lot of ways, what's happened to you is good. I mean, I know it's tough for *you*, but it's kind of a blessing for *us*."

"I still don't understand. What kind of problems were we having that—"

"Forget it," he said sharply. "That was before. What's important is where we are right now."

His rebuke unsettled her. The entire conversation was troublesome, compounding her feeling that she was an actress who had suddenly stepped into someone else's play. Too many questions and not enough answers.

He noticed her withdrawal. "I've spoiled our evening," he said.

"No, you didn't. It's me. I just can't get it right. It's . . . too much. I think we'd better go."

Calvin nodded, waved at a waiter for the bill, and they left. In front of the restaurant, Elizabeth shivered, then breathed in the cool evening air. The dusk cast a metallic blue light over the street. The restaurant's neon light buzzed overhead.

"The hospital is that way," he said, hooking his hand through her arm.

She hesitated. "Calvin . . . thank you very much for the dinner."

"Uh-oh."

"Please don't take this wrong, but . . . would you mind if I walked back to the hospital alone?"

Calvin's face tightened. "I blew it. I pushed too hard, right? I'm sorry."

Elizabeth patted his hand as she slipped her arm away. "Uh-uh. I'd just like to be alone for a little while. It's beautiful tonight, and I think it would do me a lot of good to walk back by myself."

"I'm not sure Doctor Waite would approve," Calvin said with a forced lightheartedness.

"He doesn't have to know. And I promise not to run away." She reached up and kissed him lightly on the cheek. It seemed like the correct thing to do. "Thank you, Calvin."

He shoved his hands into his pockets. "You're welcome."

She walked away, glancing back once to see him still standing under the green cursive Giovanni's sign, glowering like a little kid who'd been left behind while his friends went on vacation.

Her emotions battled against each other as she walked. *Calvin is certainly charming. I can see why Sarah went for him. But what went wrong between them?* It made sense that Calvin wouldn't want to burden her with past conflicts, but was there more he wasn't saying for other reasons?

Elizabeth realized how vulnerable she was. People could tell her anything about themselves—or about Sarah—and she'd be inclined to believe them. How would she know any better? She was never the kind of girl to second-guess people's motives. But in this situation, was that smart thinking? Maybe she should be more careful. Maybe she shouldn't be so quick to trust anyone.

Her thoughts of vulnerability and trust made her remember that she didn't know if this part of town was safe. The offices on the street were dark, the shops closed. The sidewalk was empty, and only one car and a taxi passed by. Surely Calvin wouldn't have let her walk back to the hospital if it was a bad area of town. But she'd been so adamant about going alone—maybe he didn't want to be bossy.

She looked around and was relieved to see the hospital just a couple of blocks ahead at the end of the street.

Then she was grabbed and pulled into an alley.

CHAPTER 16

Jeff had fallen asleep in front of the television. His sleep was fitful and his dreams terrifying as he saw himself waiting for hours at the Old Sawmill for Elizabeth.

He sits in the corner facing the door . . . Elizabeth walks in . . . Seeing him, she approaches slowly, reaching up to put her arms around his neck . . . He pulls her close to kiss her . . . Then she steps back, and he looks into her face . . . But it isn't her face . . . It's hardly a face at all . . . It's a skeletal blob with sunken eyes and rotting skin. . . . Jeff opens his mouth to scream, but nothing comes out except a shrill ringing . . .

The phone.

Jeff grabbed it and realized too late that he was sweating and breathing heavily. "Hello?" he panted.

"Jeff? Hi, it's Jerry Anderson from the *Gazette*."

Just then the doorbell rang.

"I want to get a statement from you—and your uncle if he's around."

"Statement?" Jeff asked. "Statement about what?"

The doorbell rang again. *Mrs. Packer must be out,* Jeff thought. Then he heard the click of Uncle Malcolm's heels against the stone floor in the front hallway.

"About Elizabeth," Jerry said, then stammered, "Uh, you have heard, haven't you?"

"Heard what?" Jeff asked.

The phone line was suddenly filled with the silence of Jerry's embarrassment. "Maybe I should talk to your uncle first."

Uncle Malcolm opened the front door, and Jeff could hear low voices. He was sure that one of them belonged to Sheriff Hounslow.

Something terrible has happened.

"Jeff?" Jerry Anderson said, his voice fading as Jeff slowly lowered the phone to his side and stared at the doorway of the room. Uncle Malcolm stood there with Sheriff Hounslow and another policeman.

"Jeff," Uncle Malcolm said. "We need to go to the hospital."

"Hello?" Jerry Anderson called again in a thin voice.

Jeff swallowed hard. "What's wrong?"

Uncle Malcolm looked at Jeff solemnly. "They found Elizabeth. She's in a coma."

CHAPTER 17

In the alley, a rough hand covered her mouth.

"Don't scream," said a man's voice. "I'm not going to hurt you."

Elizabeth struggled anyway.

The man tightened his grip and pulled her against the rough brick wall, so they were hidden from the street in a shadow. He spoke quickly. "Listen to me. You're being followed by someone. Now just stay still until we can figure out who it is and whether you're safe or not, okay?"

His grip was strong enough to make Elizabeth realize that she couldn't overpower her captor. She relaxed a little and let her mind work out a way to escape.

He kept a firm hold on her but said nothing more. Both of them were breathing heavily. They faced the street where Elizabeth had just been walking. Rapid footsteps announced someone's approach. Suddenly, framed by the edge of the two buildings at the end of the alley, Calvin appeared. Elizabeth wanted to cry out, but knew better than to try it. Calvin looked around quickly, then moved on.

"Was he supposed to be following you?" the man asked. " 'Cause I'll be honest. The way he was sneaking around behind you had me pretty worried."

Had you worried? Elizabeth thought. *You drag me into an alley with your hand over my mouth, and you're worried?*

"Let me explain," he said quickly. "I work for the hospital. I saw you in Dr. Waite's therapy group."

Oh no. I've been grabbed by one of the wackos.

As if he could read her mind, he said, "I'm not *in* the group. I just saw you there. I heard what you said—your story about being someone else. I wanted to talk to you because I understand how you feel. Maybe I can help you."

Her heart beat like a scared rabbit's. She didn't offer a response.

"Look," he said. "I'm going to let you go, and what I'd like to do is walk you back to the hospital. Will you let me do that? I'm not out to hurt you. Trust me."

Do I have a choice? she wondered. Then, figuring that cooperation might at least give her a chance to escape, she nodded her head.

Slowly he let go of her, but she was aware that his arms were ready to grab her again if she made a quick move. She turned to face him.

It was the hospital maintenance man.

"It's you," she said.

He seemed surprised. "You recognize me?"

"I saw you. You came into my first therapy meeting to clean up those dirty cups," she said. "What are you trying to pull? You scared me to death."

He hung his head repentantly. "I'm sorry. But I figured if I didn't get you fast, that guy might grab you."

"That *guy* is my boyfriend," Elizabeth snapped, then realized what she had said. "Well, sort of."

The man cocked an eyebrow. "What kind of boyfriend sneaks around like that? He sure didn't want you to know he was back there."

Elizabeth frowned. "Yeah? And why were you following me?"

"I've been trying to keep an eye on you ever since I heard your story," he said. "When I found out you left the hospital tonight, I was worried."

"Why? What do you care about me?"

"I care because . . . " He paused. "Can we get out of this alley?"

"Good idea," she said. They walked to the end of the alley, checked to see if the sidewalk was clear, then stepped out and headed for the hospital. "I wish you'd just slipped me a note or something. My heart's about to pound out of my chest."

"Mine too." He smiled. "I don't normally grab young girls in the street."

"Glad to hear it," she said, and then reminded herself that she wasn't supposed to trust people so willingly. "Okay, finish what you were saying. Why do you care what happens to me?"

"Well, I took a peek at your hospital records, and I don't believe you're a fruitcake."

"Thank you."

"Which means that you're telling the truth when you talk about not being from here—that you *do* have another life, the one you remember."

"So?"

"So, I'm here to tell you that you need to believe in those memories. They're real. Don't you let anyone tell you differently."

Elizabeth felt split down the middle. Half of her wanted to hug him in relief; the other half was angry, defensive. "How do you know?" she demanded.

"Because the same thing happened to me."

Elizabeth stopped. "What?"

"I won't get into the whole story right now. But one day I showed up here and everybody kept calling me one name, and I kept saying I had another name and, just like you, they treated me like some kind of amnesiac. Time and persistence finally made me give in. I thought, *Hey, if calling me George will help us get along, then I'll be George.* I've been George for a long, long time. So, do I call you Sarah or Elizabeth?"

Elizabeth scrunched her face up with indecision. "I haven't been here a long, long time." She gestured toward the hospital. "They think I'm Sarah, and I'm starting to believe them. So that's who I say I am. It doesn't make any sense. But I'm gonna be honest: I don't know if I should believe a word you're saying."

George chuckled low and long. "I don't blame you—especially after listening to all those stories from the folks in your therapy group. What can I say to convince you I'm not nuts?"

"I don't know if there's anything you can say to convince me," Elizabeth admitted. "You could be a dream just like everything else. But I'd like to know how I got here, if I don't really belong."

"I figured you'd ask me that," George said, scratching his temple. "I've been thinking about it for years, and I'm still not sure. I have an idea, though, if you'd like to hear it."

"Go ahead."

"First: how's your belief?" he asked.

"My belief in what?"

He smiled. "Your belief in things you can't see, things that are too bizarre for us to understand."

Elizabeth thought about her parents and their small-part-of-a-bigger-picture lectures. It was all connected to going to church, she knew, but she couldn't be sure how. She shrugged in reply.

"That'll have to do, I guess," George said. He hesitated. "I figure that we're from an alternative time, and somehow we got crossed-over to this time." He glanced at her warily.

She sighed. "I'm not a big science-fiction fan. You wanna tell me how that's possible?"

"I don't know," George confessed. "As best as I can figure, it's like switching channels on the TV. You know how sometimes if you catch two programs at the right moment, they seem to belong together? A character on channel two will say 'How are you?' and, if you switch to channel three, a character on another program says 'I'm fine, thanks.' Maybe it's like that."

"That's just a coincidence," Elizabeth argued.

"I'm a big believer in coincidences. They're the secret workings of God. You do believe in God, don't you?"

"Well . . ."

"I don't mean some fuzzy idea of God. I mean *God*. A real person. A living, loving Being who's bigger than what we know and makes plans we don't always see." By now they'd reached a side entrance to the hospital. He opened the large metal door for her.

Elizabeth thought again of her parents, their persistent trust in God and in a reality that went beyond her own. Did she really believe it? She shrugged again. "Well . . . I think so."

"You think it was a coincidence that we met? It wasn't," he said.

She eyed him uneasily. He didn't seem crazy, but how much was she expected to believe? "This is really hard to swallow. I mean, it's easier to believe that I'm just Sarah who lost her memory."

"I know, I know." George nodded sympathetically. "You have to hang on. Keep faith in the truth. I'll help you if I can. But we have to stick together."

He stepped back outside and closed the door behind him, leaving her in an empty stairwell. She wasn't sure what to think. On the one hand, she was relieved to hear that someone understood how she felt. On the other hand, she couldn't help but be alarmed that someone else was crazy enough to understand! *She* certainly wouldn't understand, if it hadn't happened to her.

"Stick together," she said aloud, her voice echoing around her. "I'm not sure I like that idea."

CHAPTER 18

Jeff nearly raced into the hospital room, but was reined in by Uncle Malcolm's firm hand on his shoulder. From the door he saw Alan and Jane Forde by the bed. A nurse was at the head, adjusting pillows. They all looked up at him as if they thought he might be a doctor with news. Alan rose to his feet but didn't speak. Uncle Malcolm gave Jeff a gentle nudge forward.

His legs felt rubbery and his shoes were like concrete slabs as he walked to the side of the bed and looked down at the figure lying there.

It was Elizabeth. She looked emaciated, her pale face stark against the white hospital gown. Her breathing was harsh and strained.

Jeff gritted his teeth to clench back the sorrow. The nurse pulled the sheet up as if tucking her in for a quiet night's sleep.

"She was found half-immersed in the river, close to the Old Sawmill," Sheriff Hounslow said from somewhere behind them.

Mrs. Forde sobbed. She was clinging to a bundle in her lap. It looked to Jeff like black sweat pants, and draped over her knees was a T-shirt with a graphic design on it.

Jeff turned his eyes back to Elizabeth. Her hair was matted, and there were dark circles under her eyes. Her throat was bruised and puffy. *What happened to you, Bits?*

Alan Forde began to whisper a prayer. Uncle Malcolm tapped Jeff on the shoulder and gestured for him to come out into the hall.

Hounslow was already there. He moved away from the doorway, speaking quietly as Malcolm and Jeff followed. "She was found by some kids who were looking for a new fishing spot. She was nearly hidden beneath an overgrowth of bushes along the edge. The current probably took her there. The searchers didn't find her because the bushes obscured everything unless you looked from just the right angle."

"What's the doctor say?" Malcolm asked.

"He figures someone tried to strangle her, then dumped her

into the river." Sheriff Hounslow dropped some coins into a coffee vending machine. "Maybe the attacker thought she was dead. Maybe he or she was interrupted. We don't know."

"Was there any other . . . physical violence?" Uncle Malcolm asked carefully.

The sheriff shook his head. "No. She was choked, nothing else. But she's in pretty bad shape. Strangled, subject to exposure by the river. . . . Doc says she might not come out of the coma."

Jeff's heart broke. He struggled to fight the burning in his eyes. "Who did it? Any ideas?"

The machine gurgled and clicked as it poured Sheriff Hounslow his cup of coffee. "No," he answered, then scrutinized Jeff's face. "Do *you* have any ideas?"

The question was fraught with suspicion, and Jeff knew right away that he was still a suspect.

"We want you to come back to the station for questioning," Hounslow said. "And by all means bring a lawyer."

The walkie-talkie on his belt came to life in a burst of static. The sheriff excused himself, grabbed his coffee, and ventured to the waiting room to talk to one of his officers.

"Don't worry," Uncle Malcolm said softly.

Jeff didn't say anything.

"I'm going back into the room to pray with Alan and Jane. Do you want to join us?"

Jeff nodded.

In the room, Uncle Malcolm and Jeff knelt next to Elizabeth's parents. The four of them held hands as each one took a turn to say as much or as little to God as they needed to. Jane clasped Jeff's hand tightly, so tightly it trembled. Jeff glanced over in time to see a tear drop onto her white knuckles, then slide down to the T-shirt still draped like a flag over her knee. *The Montfair Rock & Jazz Festival, August 12–15th*, it said—then the letters went out of focus as Jeff cried too.

"God, please make her well again," he prayed. "And catch whoever did this."

Sheriff Hounslow appeared in the room and looked expectantly at Jeff. With Uncle Malcolm right behind, Jeff followed the sheriff out of the room and down to the police station.

CHAPTER 19

"They think I tried to kill her!" Jeff said as he and Uncle Malcolm drove away from the station two hours later. Night had fallen, and a bright moon shone down on them.

"Let them think what they want," Uncle Malcolm snorted. "Unless they have solid evidence, they can't do anything but ask you questions."

"But why—" Jeff lamented, "*why* would they think—I mean, *how* could they think that I would do that to Elizabeth? I love her!" He said it before he could stop himself.

Uncle Malcolm looked over at Jeff. "Really?" His face was a psychedelic array of oranges, greens, whites, and grays from the passing street lamps and business signs.

"You know I do," Jeff said.

"Well, I always suspected you did. I was waiting for you to figure it out."

They drove on silently.

Uncle Malcolm's mind was working hard, Jeff could tell. "Hounslow is thinking about the argument you had in the diner," he eventually said.

"It wasn't really an argument," Jeff said. "I was trying to talk her out of running away."

"That's what you say . . . but all anyone else knows is that you were arguing," Uncle Malcolm said in a calm voice. "Hounslow is just drawing what seems to him to be a logical conclusion. You met Elizabeth at the Old Sawmill down by the river, the argument continued, things got out of control. In a fit of anger you grabbed her, strangled her, and threw her body into the river in panic."

"But I'd never lay a hand on her, Uncle Malcolm. Ever!" Jeff said. "Not even when we were kidding around."

Uncle Malcolm nodded. "Everyone who knows you doesn't doubt that for a minute. But Hounslow doesn't know you. And even if he did, Jeff, it's his job to consider all the possibilities."

They drove on in silence for another mile.

Uncle Malcolm sighed.

"What's wrong?" Jeff asked.

"Well, you know I'm glad Elizabeth has been found, even in her condition. At least she's alive."

"So what's wrong?"

"This blows apart my theory about how she disappeared," he said, disappointment heavy in his voice. "I thought she was a case of a genuine disappearance because of the locked bathroom. It turns out she was just another missing person."

Jeff thought for a moment. "But how *did* she get out of the locked bathroom?"

"We'll pray that she gets well enough to tell us that herself," Uncle Malcolm said.

CHAPTER 20

Morning arrived, and with it Dr. Waite. Elizabeth had just finished tying her shoes when he walked in clutching his clipboard like a life-preserver. He smiled but didn't say anything. Elizabeth looked at him, perplexed. Still he didn't speak. He just stood looking like the cat who swallowed the canary.

Elizabeth put her hands on her hips and stared at him. "Okay, I give up," she finally said.

"You can go home."

"Home?"

"I'm persuaded that you are ready to leave the hospital," he said. "You've made enough progress—not a lot, mind you, but sufficient enough to release you. Getting out of here will probably aid your recovery, particularly once you're back in your old surroundings."

Which old surroundings? she wanted to ask, but she checked the thought.

"Of course, I'll expect you to continue coming to our therapy meetings," he added. "We have a lot left to sort through."

She nodded and thought about her encounter with the hospital worker last night. *Now that crazy George,* she thought. *There's somebody for the therapy group.*

Calvin's head appeared around the corner. "Well?" he said, wearing a sheepish smile.

"Get her out of here," Dr. Waite said playfully. In a flurry of his white smock, he was gone.

"Get packed and I'll take you home," Calvin said.

Elizabeth wasn't sure. "You mean *your* home, right?"

"You don't have any other, do you?"

"But . . . are you really sure you . . . I mean . . ." She wasn't certain what she meant. Maybe her uneasiness was born out of not wanting to be an imposition. Maybe it was because she didn't want to go back there with Calvin and his iceberg parents.

Calvin streamed past her toward her suitcase. "Don't be dumb. Pack up and let's get out of here."

The drive through Fawlt Line gave her the creeps. Once again she was able to see the marked similarities and differences from the town she remembered. She closed her eyes tight and opened them again, hoping that one reality or the other would take hold. If she were Elizabeth, she wanted to be *completely* Elizabeth. If she were Sarah, then God please let her be Sarah. Just one or the other. Was it so much to ask?

"How was your walk back to the hospital last night?" Calvin asked abruptly as they passed McIntyre's Lumber Store. In *her* Fawlt Line, it had a giant plastic lumberjack on the roof.

"Okay," she said. "I was nervous when I realized that I didn't know how safe the neighborhood was." She quickly decided that telling him about Crazy George, as she'd come to think of him, wouldn't help anything. Calvin would probably get the poor man fired.

Calvin persisted, his voice strained. "Did you see anyone?"

Elizabeth swiveled in the seat to face him. "What's wrong? Why're you grilling me?"

"Because I saw you with someone!" he growled. "The two of you went in the side entrance to the hospital."

"That was just some man who opened the door for me," Elizabeth said indignantly. "What were you doing, following me?"

Calvin's knuckles were white around the steering wheel. "I was worried. I wanted to make sure you got back safe. So who is this new chum, huh?"

Elizabeth turned back in the seat to face forward and folded her arms defiantly. "I don't like being interrogated."

"But—"

"It's none of your business!"

They both nearly bumped their heads as he took the curb onto the driveway too hard. Calvin got out and stormed into the house, leaving her to get her suitcase and take it up to Sarah's room. There she closed the door and collapsed onto the bed.

Calvin in a jealous rage? It didn't match up with the charming and kind Calvin she knew. But what did she know for sure? How could she know anyone in just a couple of days? Once more, she reminded herself not to be so trusting and gullible.

There was a gentle tap on the door, and when Elizabeth spoke, Calvin came in.

"I'm sorry," he said. "I don't know why I acted like that."

Without speaking, she climbed from the bed and busied herself with unpacking.

Calvin didn't give up. "A lot has happened. I feel really stressed. I'm sorry, Sarah," he repeated. "Can you forgive me?"

Saying sorry was one thing; asking for forgiveness was another. Elizabeth had been raised to believe it was the deepest kind of apology a person could make. "Never mind," she said, smiling faintly. "You've been so nice to me. I'm sorry I upset you."

He smiled back at her. "You are different. The old Sarah never apologized for anything."

She blushed and returned to hanging up her clothes.

"Sarah," Calvin called out.

Elizabeth turned.

His smile was brighter. "See? You *are* Sarah."

Elizabeth looked away and in her own mind conceded that small victory to him. *It's so much easier this way*, she thought as she remembered Crazy George's remark about answering to the new name. *Beats being treated like a lunatic, anyway.*

Later, while Calvin was washing his car, Elizabeth dug a phone number out of her jeans pocket and slipped to the phone in the kitchen. Calvin's parents were still at work. She picked up the receiver, half-hoping to hear the voice of Helen, Fawlt Line's would-be psychic operator. There was only a dial tone. Disappointed, she punched in a number. Rhonda answered.

"It's Eli—I mean, it's Sarah. I'm out of the hospital and back at Calvin's. You said to call if I ever wanted to get out for a while. Well, I'm calling."

Rhonda was just on her way out to go shopping and said she'd be happy to pick her up.

Outside on the porch, Calvin worked unsuccessfully to mask his annoyance. "This isn't a good idea," he complained. "Dr. Waite would be against it."

"Do you want me to call him and ask?" Elizabeth offered.

Calvin retracted the statement. "No . . . but you don't remember how Rhonda is."

"How is Rhonda?"

"You two aren't good for each other," he said. "She was always a bad influence on you."

"How could I know that?" Elizabeth asked.

Calvin's face took on the same expression it had had when he was angry in the car, but this time he kept the emotion in check. "Have fun," he said through taut lips.

Rhonda arrived ten minutes later, and Elizabeth jumped into the passenger side of her small economy car. Somehow it seemed an odd match for Rhonda's sports-car personality. She was a beautiful girl with short hair and an athletic but not unfeminine build. Elizabeth had the impression that Rhonda was determined and used to having things her own way. Was that why Calvin thought she was a "bad influence"?

The girls chatted about nothing in particular until they got to Darcy Street—a stretch dedicated to stores of all kinds. Elizabeth felt envious. Her Fawlt Line didn't have a shopping district.

As they looked over a rack of blouses in a large department store, Rhonda said, "So, tell me everything about the hospital. Was it really boring, or did they stick you with a bunch of weirdoes?"

Her question was so innocently funny that Elizabeth laughed and felt comfortable enough to tell her all that had happened. She included her dinner with Calvin and the walk back to the hospital. She made a snap decision, however, not to mention Crazy George.

"Did you see anyone else at the hospital?" Rhonda asked.

"No," Elizabeth said too quickly, still thinking about the hospital worker.

Rhonda glanced up at her. "Whoa, it was just an innocent question. Why the sharp answer?"

Elizabeth pushed a group of blouses down the rack. "Because Calvin asked me the same question and got really mad." It was all she could think to say to cover her awkwardness.

Rhonda rolled her eyes. "Oh, not that again."

Elizabeth looked blank, and Rhonda took a breath. "Look, I don't want to cause problems while you two are repairing yourselves, but you'd better get used to that. Calvin's really possessive. It used to drive you nuts." She hesitated. "But you're not yourself now, are you? Maybe the new you will like it."

"It surprised me," Elizabeth said and held up a Victorian-looking blouse with a high ruffled collar. "Would the old me like this?"

Rhonda frowned and shook her head. "Not in a million years. But if you like it, get it. There are no rules about who you have to be, right? I mean, how many of us get a chance to completely reinvent ourselves?"

Elizabeth thought that was an interesting way to look at it. If she could figure out how to get some money, maybe she'd buy some new clothes.

"Nobody else visited you?" Rhonda asked, a little too casually.

"You've got someone particular in mind," Elizabeth said.

Rhonda shrugged.

"Come on," Elizabeth coaxed her. "Who are you thinking about?"

"You won't remember anyway."

"Then it won't matter if you tell me."

Rhonda didn't have a counterpoint, so she said simply, "David. I thought David would come to see you."

The name meant nothing to Elizabeth. "Sorry. No David. Who is he?"

Rhonda smiled mischievously. "No comment."

"No fair."

"Honest," she said. "You're better off leaving some things

alone—and he's one of them."

Elizabeth took her advice. A new character in this strange play would only complicate things.

They spent the rest of the afternoon shopping. Elizabeth got the feeling that it was a ritual—a test—to see if Rhonda and the "new" Sarah could be friends as they were before. For Elizabeth, the answer was yes. She liked Rhonda. There was something "big city" about her, unlike the girlfriends she was used to in Fawlt Line.

But after Rhonda dropped her off at Calvin's house that evening, Elizabeth reflected on their conversation about who else she had seen. Had Calvin also been wondering if she had seen this mysterious David? Or was it just a coincidence?

Coincidences, Elizabeth could hear Crazy George say, *are the secret workings of God.*

She walked up the dusk-lit driveway and looked at the silhouette of Calvin's somber, foreboding house. It sent a chill down her spine.

CHAPTER 21

Jeff paced from one end of Elizabeth's hospital room to the other, accompanied by the rhythmic hiss and blip of the equipment connected to the comatose girl. Step two-three, *blip* two-three.

Mr. and Mrs. Forde had gone for dinner in the hospital cafeteria. They wouldn't be away long, Jeff knew. They had suspended their lives to stay near their daughter.

A police officer, assigned to guard Elizabeth from whoever hurt her in the first place, watched Jeff warily from the hall.

Wake up, Bits, Jeff prayed. *Come on, you can do it.* He took to counting backwards from ten, like a rocket countdown, hoping she'd open her eyes when he got to one. *Lift off.*

But she lay in the same solemn state she had been in since they brought her from the river.

Carefully folded, like a flag after a state funeral, Elizabeth's clothes sat on a small table near the bed. They were the clothes she had been wearing when she was found—black sweat pants, T-shirt, and smudged white tennis shoes—except now they were washed, no doubt by Mrs. Forde. Did she think Elizabeth would want to wear them when she woke up and could go home?

Jeff picked up the T-shirt. It was black with gold cursive letters reading *Montfair Rock & Jazz Festival, August 12–15.*

A cleared throat startled Jeff, and he dropped the T-shirt back onto the table and spun around. Sheriff Hounslow stood at the edge of Elizabeth's bed.

"No change, huh?"

Jeff shook his head.

"Come on out into the hall," the sheriff said. "I want to ask you a couple questions."

Jeff didn't move. "I don't think Uncle Malcolm wants me to answer any more of your questions unless he's here."

"It's routine stuff, Jeff. Look, the more I learn, the less I'm inclined to think that you had anything to do with this. Just a couple of questions, that's all. Help me out, will you? Besides, your uncle isn't even in town."

That was true. Uncle Malcolm had flown back to Washington, D. C. for reasons he didn't explain.

Reluctantly, Jeff stepped into the hall with the law officer.

Hounslow popped a piece of chewing gum into his mouth. "Let me get this straight. You said you went into the Old Sawmill and didn't leave until we found you, right?"

"Right."

"Then why did we find your footprints along the river's edge?"

The question took Jeff back as his memory searched for an answer. Then he found one. "I had to go to the bathroom. So I went down to the river."

Sheriff Hounslow chewed his gum noisily, his jaw working machine-like. "Why didn't you say so before?"

"I didn't think about it before," Jeff answered.

"So you went down to the river to piddle," he mused. "But your footprints were up and down that part of the river's edge, like you were running. Why?"

"I thought I saw a bear on the other bank. I was sneaking up and down trying to get a look at it." Even as Jeff said spoke, he knew it sounded lame. He braced himself.

Hounslow merely offered a stiff nod. "Okay. That's all."

Jeff's relief was short-lived. The sheriff suddenly turned to him again and said, "Tell your uncle to go ahead and hire that lawyer for you. You're gonna need one."

"What?"

"This looks pretty bad, Jeff. Based on the witnesses to your fight at the diner, I'd say we have the motive. Your footprints at the river's edge, which were only a few yards from where the girl was found, certainly put you at the scene of the crime." He smiled triumphantly. "If I weren't so sure that your uncle won't let you run off, I'd arrest you now. But we have time."

Jeff gaped at him.

Hounslow nodded toward Elizabeth's room. "I don't need to tell you the mess you'll be in if she doesn't live." He walked off.

Stunned, Jeff leaned against the cold hospital wall. The police officer by Elizabeth's door smirked at him. Jeff looked away and tried to think clearly. All the same questions ricocheted around in his head. *What happened to Elizabeth that night? How did she get out of a locked bathroom? Why would she wander in her sweat pants, T-shirt, and tennis shoes to the Old Sawmill to meet him?* Jeff glanced down the hall at the retreating figure of Sheriff Hounslow. *So many questions, and he's not even trying to answer them anymore. He's sure I did it.*

The image of Elizabeth in her sweat pants, T-shirt, and tennis shoes nagged at him. There was something not quite right about it.

Ignoring the police officer, Jeff walked back into the room with its hissing and blips and stopped at the small table. The T-shirt lay crumpled where he'd dropped it. *What's wrong with this picture?*

The T-shirt. The bright gold graphic. Wait a minute. What in the world was the Montfair Rock and Jazz Festival? In all the time Jeff had known Elizabeth, he had never seen her wear that shirt or mention any rock and jazz festival. Where had the shirt come from? It was worth investigating—a small mystery that might help with the bigger one. If he couldn't pray Elizabeth awake, maybe he could do something else to help.

First things first. Who would know how to find out about the festival?

Who else but Uncle Malcolm?

Waking up in a room that was like her own, but really wasn't, put Elizabeth in the doldrums again. At least in the hospital she could consent to being Sarah without really having to *be* Sarah. But here in Sarah's room—her room—she was face-to-face with reality. She couldn't escape. This was her life now.

Dr. Waite had instructed her to go through her bedroom thoroughly. Get acquainted with it. See if anything triggered her memory: a blouse bought for a special occasion, a knickknack from a friend, a borrowed book, a report card or school paper, letters and photos. The smallest, seemingly insignificant item, could open up her mind to Sarah's life. If nothing else, it was a way to make peace with who Sarah was as a means to unite the two people into one. How did Sarah decorate, what did she wear, where did she put things?

A few moments in the closet convinced Elizabeth that Sarah didn't have very good taste in clothes. Elizabeth didn't like anything she saw.

Behind the clothes, Elizabeth found a box. She pulled it out and found the very things Dr. Waite had hoped she would find: keepsakes and paraphernalia of a life she didn't know. A small stack of report cards from Sarah's years at school. There were teacher's comments, consistent over each passing grade. Sarah was—is—quite artistic, but her organizational skills are atrocious. She is an average student.

There were notes from friends and girlfriends. One was from Rhonda, laughing over a bit of mischief she and Sarah had gotten into. Another from Calvin pleading with Sarah to forgive him for being so "clingy."

She found a book of drawings, including half-finished sketches of horses and landscapes and a fairly good likeness of Rhonda. *I'm pretty good*, Elizabeth said to herself.

A small blue book, jammed with bank statements, caught her

attention. Elizabeth was momentarily impressed that Sarah even had a bank account . . . then she discovered that the account had over fifty thousand dollars in it. "Wow," Elizabeth gasped. Tucked into a pouch at the front of the book was a copy of a will. It was Sarah's parents' will, naming her as sole heir to all they owned, their insurance, everything—to the tune of more than seven hundred thousand dollars. "Wow!" she said again.

Elizabeth glanced through the pages and found a paragraph making it clear that she couldn't touch the money until she was eighteen. Meanwhile, she was to be placed under the guardianship of the executor of the estate or whomever he designates. According to the will, the guardians get a generous allowance for taking care of her.

Typed into the blank line for her designated guardians was "Ted and Barbara Collins"—Calvin's parents. Now she understood better why she was living there, and why they put up with her when they obviously disliked her.

She dropped the papers back into the box and pulled out a yellowed newspaper clipping wrapped in plastic. There, in an unfocused black-and-white photo and smudged type, was the chronicle of John and Kathryn Bishop's death in a car accident on Route 57. It was a straightforward incident. A rainy night, a slippery road, and a truck coming too fast in the opposite direction. The photo was an anniversary picture of John and Kathryn taken the year before they died. They didn't look at all like Alan and Jane Forde. Elizabeth was grateful for that. But it didn't take away the sudden stabbing in her chest.

Elizabeth and Sarah both felt the pain, it didn't matter which one she was. Her parents, whoever they were, were gone. If she was Sarah, they were dead from a car accident. If she was Elizabeth, they were still lost to her in whatever dream true reality might lie. Her mind spun with the realization. Did her parents know she was gone, or were they living some other kind of life that had never included Elizabeth? Were they even now being treated by doctors like Dr. Waite, because they insisted they had a daughter that no one else remembered? Or maybe she was not some figment of their imagination, but was now a missing person, someone who was gone and would never come back.

Elizabeth recalled her desire to run away. It was a thoughtless, self-centered idea that didn't take into account how her mother and father might feel about losing her. And now they had. Or she had lost them. And she knew now how Jeff felt too, when his parents died. It was unbearable.

Elizabeth recklessly shoved the keepsakes back into the box and told herself that she *must* be Sarah. How else could she cope? Wasn't it better to believe that her parents were dead and gone than to believe that they were alive and tortured somewhere, somehow, without her? *You win again, Sarah,* she thought as she turned to the dresser. *Elizabeth is the dream. You are the reality.*

She rifled through the clothes that had been dropped haphazardly into the dresser drawers, stopping to fold some and stack them neatly. She would be foolish to cling to misplaced memories. She was really a girl named Sarah who had hit her head on the side of the tub and suffered amnesia. She must start her life all over again.

Methodically she worked her way from the top drawer to the bottom. She was Sarah, but a *changed* Sarah. Things would have to be different.

On her knees, she slid open the bottom drawer and pulled out the clothes. In the rear, she was surprised to find a Bible buried under some old white socks. A Bible? That wasn't consistent with the Sarah she was getting to know. She flipped it open and found color illustrations of Bible stories. Moses with the Ten Commandments. David slaying Goliath. Elijah calling down fire from heaven on the priests of Baal. Jesus gathering children on his knee. Jesus emerging from the tomb on Easter morning. Elizabeth turned the pages and found a pressed flower, brittle purple and black. *From Sarah's childhood?* she wondered. *From my childhood,* she corrected herself.

She slid the Bible toward the closet to put in the keepsake box later. It banged against the closet door, and a couple of papers that had been stuck in the back pages spilled out. One was a baptismal certificate. The other appeared to be a photograph. It was face down, and Elizabeth could see "David—Veteran's Day Picnic" written on the back. The handwriting resembled her own. Intrigued to see who this mysterious David was, she picked up the photo and turned it over.

It was a picture of a young man with curly black hair standing next to a tree. The young man was Jeff.

CHAPTER 13

Elizabeth nervously tapped the top of the table, waiting. At the other end of the cafe, someone laughed heartily. Knives and forks rattled and clattered with the coffee cups and saucers. A waitress wrote the lunch specials in Day-Glo paints on a board.

Rhonda casually looked at the photograph of David, then back at Elizabeth. "Why are you showing this to me? I know what David looks like."

"But I don't—I mean, I didn't until this morning. Now I want to know everything about him."

Rhonda smiled impishly as she sipped her soda. "Why didn't you ask Calvin? He'd have a few things to say about David."

Elizabeth frowned. "That's what I'm afraid of. That's why I'm asking you."

"Does Calvin know you're meeting me for lunch?"

"No. I don't have to tell him everything, do I?"

"You used to," Rhonda answered. "And it drove you crazy."

Elizabeth glanced across the room and saw someone who looked a lot like Calvin. It made her jump. It was true—she was afraid of Calvin's reaction if he found she had sneaked out to have lunch with Rhonda to talk about David. Elizabeth leaned forward and spoke quietly. "Rhonda, I'm really confused. You're the only one I can count on."

"Yeah, sure," Rhonda said. Then she tossed her head back and laughed. "It's so funny to hear you say that. There were times when I didn't think you ever counted on *anybody*, Sarah."

"I'm . . . different now."

Rhonda looked at Elizabeth earnestly. "I guess you are."

"So, tell me about David. It would mean a lot to me if I knew."

Rhonda ran her fingers through her short hair. It fell back into place perfectly and, for a second, Elizabeth wondered why she couldn't have hair like that. "How am I supposed to start? It's hard to just launch into who David Wilcox is."

"I don't want his whole life story," Elizabeth said impatiently. "I just want to know what he has to do with *me*."

Rhonda shook her head. "No, Sarah. It's what he has to do with all of us. See, David was my boyfriend."

"Your boyfriend!" Elizabeth exclaimed. "Then why do I have his picture hidden away like that?"

Rhonda's lips slid into a razor-thin smile. "Because you met him through me when things were bad between you and Calvin and . . . you were nuts about him . . . and you finally got him."

Elizabeth was aghast. "I *stole* him from you?"

Rhonda shrugged. "That's one way of putting it."

"You must have hated me," Elizabeth said, looking away guiltily.

"It kinda put a strain on our relationship, yeah." Rhonda fiddled with the straw in her drink.

"What happened?"

"That's the mystery. He was going to run away with you the night . . . well, the night everything changed for you."

Elizabeth nearly knocked over her soda. "Run away?"

"Yeah. You said you had figured out a way to get to your inheritance, and you were gonna leave Fawlt Line for good. That's what I thought had happened, until I heard you were in the hospital with amnesia. That's why I wasn't sure about you. I figured you were up to another one of your old tricks."

Elizabeth put her face in her hands. It was more than she could take in. The similarities between her story and Sarah's were too close to deny. If Dr. Waite was there, he'd say it was another link to show that the two of them really were the same person. "Where is David now?" she asked.

"He's around," Rhonda answered.

"Are you seeing him again?"

"Are you kidding? Not a chance."

"Will you help me?" Elizabeth asked. "Will you set it up so I can meet him?"

"Don't do it, Sarah. Forget about him. It could ruin everything all over again."

Elizabeth shook her head quickly. "No, you don't understand. I have to see him. I'll go crazy if I don't." She looked Rhonda directly in the eyes. "You have to help me."

Rhonda gazed at Elizabeth silently, then leaned back in her chair. "When you talk like that, it's just like the old Sarah."

"I don't care," Elizabeth said, undaunted. She wanted to tell Rhonda that it was because David looked like Jeff, but thought better of it. "I have to meet David, because it'll help my amnesia. Maybe something happened that night with him that made me forget everything."

Rhonda raised an eyebrow skeptically. "I'll see what I can do," she promised.

To avoid a confrontation with Calvin, Elizabeth asked Rhonda to drop her off at the end of his street. Elizabeth reached the edge of the driveway and barely noticed the man coming toward her down the sidewalk from the other direction.

"Excuse me," he said.

The voice caused Elizabeth to stop and turn.

It was Crazy George. But he was out of his hospital uniform and looked like a successful businessman in regular street clothes.

"Can you get out tonight?" he asked.

"What—?"

"Can you get out tonight to take a walk?" he repeated firmly.

"I guess so," she answered. "But why?"

"It's important."

Elizabeth gritted her teeth. "Look, I'm working real hard to figure things out right now. No offense, but your channel-switching-coincidence-mumbo-jumbo stuff doesn't help."

He didn't seem to hear her. "Just meet me out here around eight. We have to talk. It may be a matter of life and death."

"Yeah? Whose?"

"Yours."

CHAPTER 24

Uncle Malcolm rubbed his eyes wearily and wondered how long he'd been watching this last group of patients through the one-way glass. He looked at his watch. Nearly ten p.m. He should have called Jeff long before this to follow up on their conversation about the mysterious T-shirt. Malcolm had suggested that he check with Jerry Anderson at the *Gazette*.

He picked up a mug imprinted with "St. Agnes Mental Facility" and sipped the coffee. It was cold. *Nothing changes around here*, he thought. For nearly a decade, before he went to work as a reasearcher for the government, Malcolm had consulted with St. Agnes as a clinical psychologist.

James Weyhauser, a good friend and now a psychiatrist at St. Agnes', stepped into the room and closed the door behind him. His movements were jerky but precise. He reminded Malcolm of a stork. "Well?"

"Coffee's cold," Malcolm said.

"Forget about the coffee. What do you think?"

Malcolm looked again at the group of patients. They were seated in a semicircle, talking to a staff therapist about their lives and memories. "They're either insane, schizophrenic, or . . ."

"Or what?" Jim dropped into a chair next to Malcolm.

Malcolm scrubbed his chin. "That's the question, isn't it?"

Indeed it was. Jim and Malcolm enthusiastically shared an interest in unexplainable phenomena. In this case, Jim had assembled a group of people who were being treated as amnesiacs. Yet, unlike most amnesiacs with short-term or long-term memory loss, these amnesiacs seemed to have very detailed memories apart from their documented lives.

"I thought you'd be interested in this group because their so-called fictitious memories have commonalities," Jim said.

Malcolm tugged at his ear thoughtfully. "But the commonalities are actually *uncommon*. They're remembering places and events that have no point of reference in society as we know it. It's as if they've made up their own little worlds."

Jim raised a finger. "*And* their own identities in those worlds. Each of them keeps insisting that he or she is someone else. That's what intrigues me—and what made the other doctors glad to be rid of them. They think it's the same condition that leads the mentally ill to delusions of being Jesus or Napoleon. But I say this group is different."

"Where did they come from?"

"All over the country," Jim said proudly. "They were sent to me because I expressed an interest in cases like these at our annual conference last year."

"Do you think that maybe . . . they aren't deluded? Is it possible that they are who they say they are?"

Jim spread his hands. "I haven't the slightest idea. But *they* sure believe they are who they say they are."

"So what's the answer?" Malcolm asked.

"I've been waiting all night for you to say the obvious." Jim smiled.

"The obvious." Malcolm looked perplexed.

"What are you always harping about?" Jim prodded, then groaned when Malcolm didn't reply. "Time, Malcolm. You're always harping about time—how we don't understand it—how there may be more to it than our here-and-now perspective. I was betting that you'd bring it up as an explanation for these people."

Malcolm honestly hadn't thought about it. "Other lives, other times," he mumbled mostly to himself. "I toy with the idea of an alternative time. I thought I had another case in Fawlt Line, but . . ." His voice faded. Immediately he regretted referring to Elizabeth as "another case."

Jim brought their discussion back on track. "They give every appearance of being normal except that they remember lives, events, places, an entire world that's different from what we know about them. How is that possible, if they aren't psychotic or suffering from paramnesia? Have they slipped a notch and gone too deeply into their own imaginations, like an author who suddenly *lives* his books?"

"Maybe."

"If not that, then . . . what?" Jim asked as a challenge.

Malcolm sat up, his mind shifting into a higher gear, and he began to speak quickly. "Okay, let's say that these people really are remembering some other time, some other life they once had. Did they cross over from that time? If they did, how did they do it? Did they just invade someone else's brain? Or is it possible that their minds snapped in the crossover?"

"So you think they are insane? They're from another time, but lost their minds in the crossover?"

Malcolm shrugged. "Or maybe it's a . . . a physical transfer somehow." He stopped, realizing he'd reached the same point he had in his conversation with Jeff a few days before. How could someone physically switch times?

Jim ran his fingers through his hair. "There's no evidence that any of these patients are other than who their birth certificates say they are. Their families know them. If people were physically jumping back and forth in time, we'd see the difference, wouldn't we?"

"Hmm," was all Malcolm could manage as a response.

The two men sat quietly for a moment. Finally, Jim clapped his hands on his knees and stood up. "Let's try the drug."

"What drug?" Malcolm rose and followed his friend to the door.

"We've been developing it in one of our labs in California," Jim explained as they walked. "It's an experimental mixture that's supposed to tap into a patient's subconscious dream-state without sending the patient to sleep. Kind of like sodium amobarbital."

"Or hypnosis?"

"Except hypnosis and sodium amobarbital can only go so far into a person's psyche. They rely on a person's memories. This drug, if the experiments are reliable, uses a modified form of the hormone norepinephrine to stimulate the part of the brain stem where we believe the subconscious, dreams, feelings of *dèjá vu*, that sort of thing, are located. The *pontine tegmentum*."

"Thanks for not boring me with details," Malcolm said. "It hasn't been *that* long since I worked here."

Jim smiled. "Anyway, it lets a person enter into the realm of dreams—not memory, mind you—and allows us to talk to him while he's there."

They walked down a hallway, jogged left, then right into a corridor. Malcolm felt like a rat in a maze.

"Does this drug have a name?" Malcolm asked.

"Well, if it works, I was thinking of calling it the Weyhauser Drug."

"Catchy," Malcolm said.

Calvin's parents escaped to watch television while Elizabeth and Calvin cleared the dinner dishes. It had been her first meal with the entire family, and she prayed it would be the last. Except to ask her to pass the butter, they didn't speak to her. Even Calvin seemed lost in a broody silence, broken only when she asked him about his day at the bank. He told her a lot more than she wanted to know about the stock exchange.

"How was *your* day?" Calvin asked when the last of the dishes were put in the dishwasher.

Elizabeth looked away self-consciously. "It was okay. I followed doctor's orders and looked through my room."

"Find anything interesting?" he asked. But it was a fake question, Elizabeth could tell. He was leading her. Somehow he already knew the answer.

"Nothing that helped me remember anything," she answered.

Her back was to him as she rinsed out a pan, but she felt his eyes on her.

"Did you go out today?" he asked.

She dropped the pan in the bottom of the sink with a bang. "Sorry," she said. "It slipped."

Calvin's voice was taut. "Y'know, I'm not sure you should go out. I don't think Dr. Waite wants you wandering around town alone."

But I wasn't alone. You know I wasn't alone. You know I was with Rhonda. Were you following me again?

Calvin continued, "You should wait until I come home, and we'll go out together."

"But I like to be alone," Elizabeth said.

"It's not good for you," Calvin snapped.

She recognized the angry tone in his voice, and it frightened her. *How can I tell him that I want to take a walk without him tonight?*

"You worry too much," she said pleasantly and walked out.

He followed her as she walked toward the living room. Seeing his parents, she made a hasty turn to go up the stairs to her room.

"Where did you go today?" he demanded.

"Calvin, what's wrong with you?"

"Nothing's wrong with me. I just asked a simple question."

Elizabeth turned on him. "What happened the night I lost my memory?"

The question stopped him cold. "What?"

"I'm trying to put the pieces together, and it would help a lot if you'd tell me what happened that night." They were in her room now.

"You're just changing the subject," he said angrily.

She folded her arms. "You're right. So how about telling me. You said at the hospital that I went to the movies alone."

He leaned against the door frame and shoved his hands into his pockets. "I made that up so the doctor wouldn't start asking a lot of embarrassing questions."

"Embarrassing for whom? You or me?"

"Both of us."

"Where did I go, Calvin?"

"You said you were going to run away—and that's what you did. You left. I thought you meant it this time." He hesitated. "Until you showed up later. Boy, was I surprised. And then I was even more surprised when you didn't know who you were."

His anger had subsided now. The memory of that night seemed to have made him anxious about losing her again, just as she had known it would. She wondered if Sarah used to manipulate him the same way.

"Where did I go that night?" she asked.

Calvin chewed his lower lip. "I don't know. You didn't tell me what you were plotting to do."

"Calvin!" his mother called from downstairs.

"Yeah?" he called back.

"Is it too much to expect you to wipe off the table?"

He rolled his eyes and jerked away from the door frame. "No,

Mom. I'll be right down." He ambled away.

Elizabeth glanced at her clock. It was twenty past eight. She went to the window and looked out into the night. If Crazy George was out there, she couldn't see him. She felt bad that she couldn't go out to meet him, but she didn't dare suggest to Calvin that she take a walk alone. He would go through the roof.

The moon and clouds cast shifting shadows on the street at the end of the driveway. The effect almost made her believe she could see someone standing down there. She sighed and turned away from the window. A matter of life and death, Crazy George had said. She tried to shrug it off. He'd only give her another lecture about TV channels anyway.

She threw herself onto her bed, and her eye was caught by a picture on the night stand. It was of her and Calvin eating cotton candy at a carnival.

What went on the night I ran away? she wondered. *I ran away and then came back without my memory. Where did I go in the meantime? What happened to me?*

CHAPTER 26

Sheriff Hounslow threw the morning edition of the *Gazette* onto the table and scowled. "It's ridiculous!" he said as he navigated his sturdy frame into a chair. "If that boy thinks he's going to get off as my prime suspect because of a rock and jazz festival, he has another think coming."

Hounslow was referring to Jerry Anderson's column about the mystery of Elizabeth's T-shirt. The newspaper had done a thorough check into the Montfair Rock and Jazz Festival and couldn't find it anywhere. It didn't exist.

Officer Peterson, Hounslow's right-hand man, scratched his bald head. "I've looked everywhere too. No one anywhere has ever heard of the Montfair Rock and Jazz Festival."

"So someone made it up," Hounslow growled. "The T-shirt was a joke."

"Mr. and Mrs. Forde said they'd never seen the shirt before. And since Mrs. Forde always did Elizabeth's laundry, she's sure she would've—"

"I know, I know, I was *there*, remember?" The chair complained as Hounslow tilted back onto its rear legs. "This is getting sloppy. I *hate* sloppy cases. Jeff's just trying to divert us from what really happened that night."

Peterson took a donut out of the open box on the table. "What do *you* think really happened?" He bit into the thick chocolate.

Hounslow clasped his hands behind his head and rocked gently in the creaking chair. "Easy. It was Jeff who really wanted to run away. Elizabeth agreed, but changed her mind. While her parents were at their church meeting, she went down to the Old Sawmill to tell Jeff that she wouldn't leave with him. Otherwise, she'd have brought clothes with her, right? Jeff got mad and tried to force her to go. She refused. That made him angrier, and he lost control."

Peterson spoke through a mouth full of donut. "Jeff Dubbs is one of the most laid-back kids in town. No one who knows him will believe that he did something like that."

"It's not my job to persuade anyone of anything—except the district attorney. I just have to come up with a plausible solution to this case. Jeff was there. We found his footprints and nobody else's, so that makes him the *only* one there." He dropped the chair back down onto four legs and considered the donut box.

"But you don't have *her* footprints there either."

Hounslow scowled. "He strangled her in the mill and carried her down."

"It's all circumstantial," Peterson said. Then he added reckless-ly, "Are you sure you don't have it in for the boy? This isn't some kinda payback because Malcolm wouldn't support you in the election last year?"

"No!" Hounslow hoisted himself to his feet. "I don't think that way, and I don't want to hear anyone suggest it. I'm interested in the facts, no more and no less."

Sally, the station's phone receptionist, tapped on the door and walked in without waiting for an answer. "Kevin on line one," she said and retreated like a cuckoo in a cuckoo clock.

Kevin was the officer watching Elizabeth's room that afternoon.

Hounslow picked up the phone and punched the button. "What's up, Kevin?"

"You need to come down here right away," the youthful voice answered.

"Why?"

"The doctor was just here talking to Mr. and Mrs. Forde and the Dubbs kid. He said he went back over Elizabeth's X-rays and found something he can't explain."

"What's that?"

"Her dental work is different," he said.

"What?"

"Her dental work is different. Elizabeth had perfect, cavity-free teeth. They've got the records to prove it. But the girl in the coma has a three-year old filling in one of her molars."

Hounslow frowned. "I don't get it. Her fingerprints are identical. Her parents—everyone—who has seen the girl has given positive identification. What's her dental work have to do with anything?"

"I'm just telling you what the doc said," Kevin stated. "Everything checks out except her teeth. Her parents and her dentist say there's no way she ever had a filling." Kevin paused for a moment. "They're saying this girl may not be Elizabeth."

Hounslow slammed the phone down.

CHAPTER 27

"Thanks, Jeff," Malcolm said and placed the phone receiver back on the cradle. The afternoon sun streamed through the half-closed blinds on the window. His head ached from too little sleep and too much thinking. He and Jim had been up late the night before testing the "Weyhauser Drug" on two of the patients. Apart from rambling stream-of-conscious talking about their dreams and fantasies, the tested drug didn't give Malcolm or Jim any new information.

"News?" Jim asked from across his desk.

"Elizabeth—the girl I told you about—may not be Elizabeth," he said.

"What's that supposed to mean? Either she is or she isn't."

Malcolm tugged at his ear. "Not necessarily. From all appearances she is. But they found an inconsistency with her dental records that they can't explain—the sudden appearance of a filling she never had. And they still haven't been able to explain the T-shirt she was wearing when they found her."

"The rock festival," Jim nodded.

"This is a very strange situation," Malcolm said.

Jim smiled. "Well, you know weird better than anyone. Come on, it's two o'clock."

"What happens at two?"

"I want you to meet a patient we brought in this morning."

The patient, Malcolm learned on the way to the interview room, had been brought to a clinic in Detroit by his wife. After several weeks of examinations, the staff psychiatrist suggested they go to St. Agnes to meet with Jim Weyhauser.

"He's nonviolent," Jim told Malcolm at the door. "Just confused. He claims to be a man named Frank O'Mara. But all his records, wife, family, and friends say he's William Putnam. Frank O'Mara says he's a mechanic, while William Putnam is an attorney. His wife, Delores, found him in the car in the garage, just sitting there, claiming not to recognize anyone or anything. He kept saying that everything was familiar, but not . . . right." The interview room was comfortably arranged to look like a cross between a board room and someone's den. Jim introduced Malcolm and Frank/William. The patient could have been Anyman from Anytown. Thinning hair, trim mustache, nondescript mouth and nose. Put him in a suit and he could be an attorney. In a smock, he might be a butcher or a baker. In overalls, a farmer or, yes, a mechanic. The only difference was his eyes. They were wide and startled, like a deer caught in the headlights of an oncoming truck.

They settled into their chairs and, after some idle chit-chat, Jim took the lead. "I've told Malcolm the basic facts about your case," he said. "Malcolm's a doctor too. A clinical psychologist."

Frank/William glanced at Malcolm nervously. "It must sound insane to you."

"Not at all." Malcolm shook his head and picked up Frank/William's file. It contained all the details of the case, medical and dental records, and a separate folder filled with X-rays. He leafed through the papers casually. "I'm curious about where you were found. Your wife said you were just sitting in your car in the garage. Do you remember why?"

"No," Frank/William answered. "All I remember was that I was driving home from work and swerved to miss a pedestrian who had suddenly stepped into the road. I headed straight for a telephone pole. I figured, 'This is it, I'm a goner.' I even figured I'd died and gone to heaven, 'cause I found myself sitting in a real nice car in a nice garage. Y'know, I'm a mechanic—I figured, what the heck, it's mechanic's heaven. Then this strange woman came out and asked me what I was doing. That's when this whole amnesia business started."

"For argument's sake," Malcolm said, "let's say that I believe you really are Frank O'Mara. Tell me what you remember about your world—the place you remember *before* you woke up in the garage."

Frank looked uneasily at Malcolm and Jim. "Dr. Carson, my therapist, said that world doesn't exist, and it's not good for me to talk about it. He said I'm an amnesiac because something awful happened and gave me a nervous breakdown. Job stress probably. I'm supposed to be a lawyer, you know."

Malcolm spoke as soothingly as he could. "Play along with me anyway, Frank. Tell me what you remember."

For the next hour and a half, Frank described his life in a town called Detroit. But the Detroit he knew was different from the Detroit he knew now. He was a mechanic who ran his own repair business. He had a wife and two sons—John and Patrick—and here he wept uncontrollably, because his memories of them were so clear. He wept as one who was grieving over the deepest loss imaginable.

Malcolm glanced at Frank/William's records and noted the conclusions of Dr. Carson. He had written that William's desire to be a mechanic might be the result of inordinate stress at his attorney's office, brought on by a major case against corrupt union officials. Dr. Carson also speculated that, since William was childless and had always wanted children, his fantasy of being the father of two boys wasn't surprising.

It's all so neat, Malcolm thought cynically. *We have it all figured out. Everything can be explained by our doctors. An open-and-shut case of paramnesia.*

Having run out of things to say, Frank fell into a melancholy silence.

"How about dreams? What kinds of dreams did you have before this happened?" Malcolm asked.

"Dreams?"

"Dreams while you slept, nightmares, anything like that."

Frank thought about it for a minute. "I have a lot of nightmares now, but nothing weird before that."

"Any odd moments while you were awake? Vivid daydreams, *dèjá vu*—"

"Day-zha what?"

"It means 'already seen,' " Malcolm explained. "It's the phrase we use to describe the feeling that we've done something before, even though we're doing it for the first time."

Frank's eyes lit up. "Yeah," he replied. "That used to happen to me a lot. It started to drive me crazy after a while." He looked down at the table thoughtfully and mumbled, "I guess it really did drive me crazy."

Jim escorted Frank/William back to his room. After a few minutes, he returned to Malcolm. "Fascinating, huh?"

"I don't know where to begin," Malcolm said. He had spread the contents of Frank/William's folder across the table. "Did you see the way he cried when he talked about his wife and children? They were real to him. I'm having a hard time believing this is some kind of mental problem."

"Then what is it?"

Malcolm waved a hand over the reports. "It's all here. Right under our noses. He isn't William Putnam, he is Frank O'Mara. He really is who he thinks he is."

"You're kidding."

"Why not? Rather than make him conform to who we think he is, why don't we accept for a minute that he is who he thinks he is?"

"I'm interested," Jim said, slipping into a chair. "Keep talking."

"Somehow, Frank O'Mara slipped from another time and place into our time and place," Malcolm said.

Jim grinned. "And what? Took over William Putnam's body? That's straight out of *The Exorcist*."

"Not at all," Malcolm said and held up the file of X-rays. "He didn't take over William Putnam's body. He brought his own body with him."

Jim looked at Malcolm silently for a moment. Then he said: "But Mrs. Putnam knows him. And his fingerprints, birthmarks—they're all the same."

Malcolm tugged at his ear. "But they're *not* all the same. The physical examination of Frank O'Mara shows that he has a scar on the back of his hand. William Putnam didn't have a scar there. How does someone instantly create a scar?" He grabbed the file and slid it across the table at Jim. "William Putnam had heart problems, Frank O'Mara doesn't. Putnam had his wisdom teeth removed twelve years ago. Frank O'Mara shows no sign of that operation—his wisdom teeth lie dormant beneath his gums. How did all the doctors miss this?"

"They didn't miss it, they ignored it," Jim said. "They had to. How do you explain it otherwise? Somebody made a mistake with the records, is what they probably thought."

Malcolm shook his head and thought about Elizabeth. "It's no mistake."

"Okay, bright boy," Jim jabbed. "You're saying that somehow Frank O'Mara physically slipped into our time from some other time. What is that other time: another universe? A parallel time?"

"Why not?"

Jim slung a leg over the side of the chair and folded his hands across his belly. "And you're saying that this Frank O'Mara, by an astronomical coincidence, is an identical twin to William Putnam?"

"Except for things like scars or dental work, yes." Malcolm knew quite well how stupid this conversation sounded.

"Then what happened to William Putnam when Frank O'Mara suddenly showed up? Where did he go? Was he obliterated by the . . . the . . ." Jim struggled for words, then said, "alternative time twin, or is he now in the other time being treated like a crazed Frank O'Mara?"

Malcolm's head throbbed. "Probably."

"And how did this sudden switch take place?"

"Is it possible that it happens through a dream state? Maybe *dèjá vu* has something to do with it. You heard Frank say he experienced it a lot. Maybe that's the door through which a physical transfer took place."

Jim sat silently and gazed at Malcolm. "Do you really believe this stuff?"

Malcolm nodded.

Thoughtfully, Jim looked at the ceiling. "Yep," he said. "It sounds right to me. But they'll lock us both up if we breathe a word of it to anyone."

CHAPTER 28

Elizabeth stood on the front porch of the Collinses' house waiting for Rhonda to pull up. She held onto the rail so tightly that her fingers ached.

This afternoon she would meet David.

A car turned in to the drive, but it wasn't Rhonda. It was Calvin. What was he doing here? Elizabeth had worked hard to avoid a scene with him before he left for the bank that morning.

He got out of the car and sprinted to the porch cheerfully. "Hi, Sarah! Guess who got the afternoon off?"

She forced a smile. "How many guesses do I get?"

"My supervisor has a bunch of meetings the rest of the day, and there really wasn't anything for me to do, so they set me free. I thought I'd steal you away for the rest of the day." He smiled at her, but she couldn't see his eyes behind the sunglasses.

Her heart sank. "Oh, Calvin. I wish you'd called first. I made other plans."

"Other plans?" His smile faded.

"I'm . . . well . . ." she stammered, "I'm meeting Rhonda this afternoon."

"Rhonda!"

"She's helping me a lot, Calvin. Dr. Waite says—"

Calvin slammed his hand against the rail. "How can Rhonda help you? What can she tell you that I can't?"

"Nothing, but—"

"I've been patient with you—more than patient, I think!" he shouted. "I keep waiting for our relationship to get back to the way it was. Has it? You don't want to be with me. You won't even let me hold your hand!"

Elizabeth fidgeted uncomfortably. "I'll leave if it bothers you that much. I saw my bank statement. I can go."

The mention of her money brought surprise to Calvin's face. He held up his hands as if surrendering. "No, wait. That's not what I meant. I just wish I could make you understand how I feel, Sarah. I . . . I don't want to lose you again."

"Then give me some room, okay? Crowding me in won't make me care for you any sooner." She answered not as Elizabeth, but as Sarah. She'd say whatever she had to say to meet David. That's what Sarah would do. Yet inside, it was Elizabeth who longed to see Jeff—even if this guy was only a bizarre replica of Jeff.

It worked. The anger receded from Calvin's face, and his jaw relaxed. He reached out and lightly touched her arm. "Promise me we'll have a day together soon. Maybe we could go to Watkin's Park. That was one of your favorite places. Maybe it would help your memory."

Rhonda pulled up just then and tapped her horn. Before there was a chance to argue or discuss, Elizabeth raced down the porch steps. "See you later," she called over her shoulder. "Don't save dinner for me!"

He waved halfheartedly, then went into the house.

Elizabeth climbed into the car and exhaled long and loud.

"An unexpected encounter?" Rhonda said coolly.

"Yeah."

"You're sure you wanna go through with this?"

Elizabeth turned to Rhonda. "It's the only thing I've been sure about since I got here."

They drove into town, and Rhonda dropped Elizabeth off in front of the same cafe where they had met before. Rhonda wouldn't stay. She made it clear that she was not interested in seeing David again.

"Thanks for setting this up," Elizabeth said.

"I'm not sure I'm doing you any favors," said Rhonda bitterly. Then she drove away.

Elizabeth scanned the restaurant as she entered. It was crowded with young people—high school and college students—as it had been the day before and probably would be tomorrow. Her heart skipped a beat when she saw him sitting in a corner booth. Jeff. She wanted to run to him and cry in his arms and then wake up and know that this whole experience had been nothing but a long, horrible dream. Instead she restrained herself and walked casually to the booth, aware of how she might look to him in the cream-colored pullover and jeans. He was a stranger to her, she told herself. A stranger.

He looked up at her without smiling, and she instantly felt his aloofness. It was Jeff looking at her, but with an expression she had never seen on his face. These eyes were cold.

"Hi," she said as she slid into the seat across from him—fighting desperately the urge to burst into tears.

He stared at her while she settled in. "What do you want?"

His bluntness hurt her. Jeff never spoke like that. *But this isn't Jeff*, she told herself again. *It isn't Jeff.* "I guess you heard what happened to me."

"I heard. But I'm not sure whether to believe it. I figure it might be one of your stunts to cover for what you did to me. Leave it to you to come up with some stupid story about remembering another life."

A waitress arrived and took their orders for lemonade, then hustled off again.

"What did I do to you?" Elizabeth asked breathlessly, not sure she wanted to hear the answer.

"Oh, come off it," he said, and slid toward the edge of the booth.

Instinctively she reached across the table for him. "Wait, please. Don't go. I don't know what you're talking about. I don't know *anything*. You have to believe me. It's not a stunt."

He settled back into his seat and looked at her skeptically. "Okay, I'll play along. You were going to leave Calvin and meet me at the Old Sawmill by the river."

"The Old Sawmill?" she gasped.

"Oh, you remember that, huh?"

"It's the only thing I remember," she answered.

Again, he looked at her as if he didn't believe a word she said. "You were supposed to meet me there. But it was do or die."

"Do or die?"

"We agreed that if you didn't show, our relationship was over."

"Why did we say that?"

"Because I was tired of your games," he said. "You kept going back and forth between Calvin and me. You wouldn't make up your mind. So I said, 'This is it. Now or never.' I waited for two hours, and you never came. I promised myself I wouldn't see you again. I'm only here to find out if this whole amnesia thing is some kind of trick."

The waitress brought their glasses of lemonade. Elizabeth picked hers up, but her hand was shaking so badly that she put it down again.

"It's no trick," she whispered. "It's no trick."

David softened at the sight of her fragility . . . a quality he had never seen in Sarah. "Then why meet with me?" he asked. "You don't remember me. Why bother?"

She fumbled in her handbag for a moment, then pulled out the photo of him she had found in the Bible. He looked at it indifferently. "Yeah? So?"

"So . . ." It was too late. The tears had come and would not be stopped. "You look exactly like someone I knew in my other memories."

David's wall of skepticism seemed to crumble. He left his seat, came around to her side of the table, and slid in next to her. She buried her face in his shoulder, and he put his arm around her and pulled her close.

From across the street, half hidden by a phone booth, Calvin watched.

CHAPTER 29

Elizabeth spent the rest of the afternoon with David. She knew it wasn't really Jeff, but she wanted to stay near him all the same. He took her to Magnolia Park—an acre of trees and well-kept gardens and arteries of zigzagging paths filled with joggers, bicyclists, playing children, and lovers on blankets. In *her* Fawlt Line, the old bank sat where this park was. This Fawlt Line was more city-like than the one she knew.

David told her about his life at a private boarding school. His parents, who according to him were too rich to pay him any attention, had put him there to get rid of their guilt. He told Elizabeth how he had met her—Sarah, that is—at another friend's birthday party. The party got out of control, so David, Sarah, and Rhonda had slipped back to Rhonda's house. "What a pair you were. You kept me laughing all evening," he said with a smile. "I fell for you right then and there."

"Weren't you already going out with Rhonda?" Elizabeth asked.

David laughed as if she were joking. "What do you mean?"

"Rhonda said that I stole you away from her."

David looked completely puzzled. "Rhonda and I were never a couple. You must have misheard her."

Elizabeth was sure that she hadn't, but she didn't say so. Why would Rhonda lie to her? Or was David the one lying?

CHAPTER 30

"This is nuts!" Jeff cried out. He and Uncle Malcolm were in the den at the cottage. "Time twins . . . alternate worlds . . . it sounds crazier than all that other junk you told me."

"It's the only explanation that makes sense. I defy anyone to explain the dental work and the mysterious rock festival on that girl's T-shirt," Malcolm said.

"*That girl* is Elizabeth," Jeff said.

"Maybe not. Even the doctor is confused about—"

"Do me a favor, okay?" Jeff interrupted. "When they arrest me, don't bring any of this up at the trial. I mean it, Uncle Malcolm. They won't even bother with a jury. They'll certify us both and send us far, far away."

"You're not getting it," Malcolm lamented.

"No, I'm not."

Uncle Malcolm spoke firmly and slowly. "The girl in the hospital is *not* Elizabeth. I thought you'd be happy to hear that."

"Why would that make me happy?"

"Because that means she may be alive and well in another time!"

Jeff again felt the heat from a tiny spark of hope. He dumped the cold water of reason on it right away, reminding himself how deranged the whole idea was.

Uncle Malcolm went on, "If they're time-twins and they swapped places, maybe through a dream-state or *déjà vu*, then maybe she's alive in an alternative time. You know what *déjà vu* is, right?"

"Yeah, I know," Jeff said. "I get it all the time."

Uncle Malcolm was surprised. "Really? You never told me."

Jeff shrugged impatiently. "Why would I?"

"No reason, I guess. Did Elizabeth?"

"Beats me," Jeff replied. "It's not something we talked about."

Uncle Malcolm looked disappointed. "Too bad."

Jeff threw his hands heavenward. "Uncle Malcolm, *please!*"

"Okay, okay." He lifted both hands in a gesture of defense. "Let's pretend for a minute that Elizabeth passed through a doorway of time—whatever it is—at some point in the evening she disappeared. While she took a bath, is my guess."

"Why then?" Jeff asked, still not believing any of it.

Uncle Malcolm tugged at his ear. "Because of the patients I saw at St. Agnes. They all have a common link between their last memory and how they were found. Frank O'Mara was in his car driving home; his "twin" William Putnam was sitting in a car in his garage. Maybe he had just pulled in. Anyway, the car is the link."

"What's that have to do with Elizabeth?"

"Elizabeth had a bath; the comatose girl was found by the river. They were both immersed in water. That's a pretty solid link. What else do we know?"

"I don't know anything," Jeff moped and folded his arms. His uncle was on a tangent and there was nothing to do but ride it out.

"O'Mara was headed for a life-threatening situation when he switched with Putnam."

Jeff frowned. "Hold it. You said Putnam was sitting in his car in the garage. That doesn't sound life-threatening to me."

Undaunted, Uncle Malcolm went on. "Maybe both sides don't have to be in a life-threatening situation when the switch happens. Though Putnam had a heart condition. Maybe he had a heart attack when he pulled into his garage."

"That's a real stretch, Uncle Malcolm."

"I know it's a stretch, but I only have half the story. I can't say what happened to Putnam on the other side. Who can? The people in the alternative time might notice the change in his dental work or scars or the sudden appearance of a heart condition, but they'd write it off as an unsolvable mystery because the fingerprints are identical. Poor William Putnam is probably being treated there the same way Frank O'Mara is being treated here. Like a lunatic."

Jeff winced. "Which means that wherever Elizabeth is, assuming this crazy idea is true, they're probably treating her the same way. Are you trying to make me feel better?"

"I'm trying to get at the *truth*, Jeff," Uncle Malcolm snapped. He continued to work through his theory. "The girl from the alternative time must have been in a life-threatening situation and switched with Elizabeth when Elizabeth was in a relaxed mental state in the bath." He stopped and suddenly buried his face in his hands.

"It's crazy, Uncle Malcolm."

"Why is it so crazy?"

"Because, if it's true, why don't people keep switching back and forth all the time, popping on and off like light bulbs?"

Uncle Malcolm ran his fingers through the hair on the sides of his head, and when his face reappeared, he was smiling at Jeff. "You're thinking," he said. "You're working it through. That's a very good question."

Jeff felt like a student who'd just been patted on the head. "Thanks, but what's the answer?"

"I don't know," Malcolm said. "Maybe there are only a handful of people with time twins. And perhaps the specific circumstances for a switch are so exact that it rarely ever happens. How many life-threatening situations do any of us *really* encounter? Not many."

"So this isn't going to help us," Jeff said.

"Maybe not," Uncle Malcolm admitted with a deep sigh. "I don't know how to prove any of it. Even if I could, it wouldn't help us cure whoever the girl in the coma is—or bring Elizabeth back."

The thought hung in the air between them, creating a cloud of despair.

Uncle Malcolm suddenly frowned. "There's something I just realized. If the comatose girl from the other time was injured because someone tried to kill her . . ."

". . . and Elizabeth is in the alternative time alive . . ." Jeff continued.

"Then whoever hurt the comatose girl is in for a big surprise."

Jeff's mouth fell open. "Not only will they be in for a big surprise . . . they may try to kill her again!"

120

Calvin dropped Elizabeth off at the hospital for her therapy group the next afternoon. He'd been in a quiet mood ever since the previous day, and she couldn't help but wonder if he somehow knew about David. But how could he know?

"You have cab fare for the ride home?" he asked.

She held up a small wad of cash he had given her. "Right."

"I'll see you back at the house. You'll be home tonight, I hope."

She nodded. She and David hadn't made any specific plans to see each other again. She only knew that she *would* see him somehow. He was a lifeline to her, even if he wasn't really Jeff.

Calvin wouldn't look at her, fixing his gaze instead on the line of cars parked ahead. She wanted to break his mood, but she didn't have the time or the inclination to play that game. It scared her to think how good she might become at manipulating him. *Is that how Sarah coped*, she wondered, *manipulating him in and out of moods?*

He rubbed his hands against the steering wheel as she closed the passenger door. His quietness made her suspicious. *It's as if he's made a decision, resolved something in his mind that he won't tell me about.*

She made it as far as the main elevator in the hospital when she was joined by Crazy George. He stood next to her at the door as if he were just another would-be passenger. The bell chimed, the arrow lit up, and the doors opened. They both stepped in.

After the door closed, he turned to her. "I've been looking for you."

Elizabeth didn't face him. "I'm sorry I didn't come out the other night. I couldn't."

"Couldn't or didn't want to?" he said sharply.

She frowned. "What's the big deal?"

"Something is going to happen. Everything in my bones tells me that a change is about to take place again."

The elevator stopped, and an orderly stepped in. She smiled at

121

them both, then faced the doors. They all waited in silence until the next floor, then Elizabeth and George stepped off.

"What kind of change?" Elizabeth asked as they walked toward her meeting room. "What are you talking about?"

"The last time I felt like this was the night you had your amnesia: the night Sarah became Elizabeth—or vice versa."

Elizabeth rolled her eyes. "A feeling in your bones . . . switching TV stations . . . why should I believe any of this stuff?"

"You should believe me because I believe you," he said. "You're no more Sarah Bishop than I am Abraham Lincoln. Now listen to me. Something is going to happen, things are going to change. Meet me tonight. We need to stay close."

"It's impossible," Elizabeth said as firmly as she could. "I can't get out tonight, and I wouldn't want to anyway. This whole thing is nutty." Before he could reply, she spun on her heel and barged into the therapy room.

Dr. Waite and his collection of the maladjusted smiled happily at her.

I'm in pretty poor shape when this group is my only escape, she thought.

After an hour of verbal spewing and nonsensical stream of consciousness, the group broke for coffee. Elizabeth was the first one out the door. She made her way to the front of the hospital, hoping she wouldn't run into Crazy George again, and went to the curb to hail a taxi. Instead, a car horn honked at her, and she found Rhonda waiting in her car across the street. "Need a lift?"

Elizabeth dodged the commuters to climb in the passenger side of the little roller skate.

"How did you know I was here?"

Rhonda guided the car into the lane. "I called the house and talked to Mrs. Collins. I figured I'd drive down and wait for you."

"Thanks," Elizabeth said. "What's up?"

"I want to know how your time with David went," Rhonda said bluntly. "I didn't think you'd be able to talk at home."

Elizabeth put her sunglasses on to ward off the late afternoon sun. "You can be sure of that."

"Well?"

Elizabeth wasn't sure how much to tell her. "It was good to see him. We had a nice talk."

"Anything else?"

"Like what?"

Rhonda smiled. "Like, you know, the old flame, the old feelings. Did he kiss you?"

"No," Elizabeth said. "I got a little worked up and cried once, so he put his arm around me. That was all."

"But you want to see him again," Rhonda said.

"Yeah, but it's not the way you think it is," Elizabeth stated. "It's different."

Rhonda turned her doubt into a tease. "Sure, Sarah. Who said it'd be different—you or him?"

"What are you talking about?"

"He's not what he seems," she answered, her tone now very serious. "He's cruel and dangerous."

"He was very nice to me."

"You went to meet him that night, and you lost your memory. If I were you, I'd wonder why."

Elizabeth shook her head. "If anything happened to me, it didn't happen because of David. He said I never showed up that night."

"He might be lying," Rhonda countered. "Maybe he did something to hurt you that night—something that *gave* you amnesia."

Elizabeth glanced out of her window at the passing cars on the ribbon of street. It looked like a black river. She had a sudden flash of that moment in the tub when it felt as if someone was strangling her, holding her under the water. It was the first time she'd thought about it since that night. The memory was so vivid that she gasped and closed her eyes tightly to shut it out.

"What's wrong?" Rhonda asked worriedly. "Are you all right? Should I pull over?"

"No," Elizabeth whispered. "It's okay. Just take me home."

Rhonda watched her from the corner of her eye. "Sarah?"

Elizabeth settled back into the seat and stared at nothing. The bath, the murky water, the strong hands left a thick residue on her feelings. She was suddenly transparent and vulnerable all over again. David . . . Rhonda—why would either of them lie to her? *Why?* she wanted to ask Rhonda. *Why do you think David hurt me the night I lost my memory? Why would anyone want to hurt me?*

But aloud she said only, "I have a headache."

"Look," Rhonda said, "I'm sorry. I just thought you ought to be warned about David. He's not who you think he is."

But not one of you is who I think you are, Elizabeth thought. *Rhonda plants seeds of doubt about David, Calvin buries an uncontrollable jealousy, David is a mystery. Who's lying? Who's telling the truth? What did I do to deserve friends like these?*

For a moment, she was torn. It was as if Elizabeth were standing directly across from Sarah, the two looking at each other skeptically with folded arms.

Who are you really? What happened to you that night?

The Sarah in her mind smiled mischievously. *You're in over your head. This is my world, and you don't belong here.*

It was the only truth Elizabeth understood. *I don't belong here.*

She managed a faint smile and thanked Rhonda for the warning. "I'll be careful."

CHAPTER 32

The more Uncle Malcolm thought about it, the more he realized that Jeff was right. Elizabeth was likely in danger at the hands of whoever tried to kill her time-twin. *If she isn't already dead*, he thought, then quickly dismissed the idea. He picked up the phone and dialed a number.

"Jim?" he said when his friend answered.

"Hi, Malcolm."

He skipped the usual pleasantries. "I need a favor."

"What kind of favor?"

It took some doing, and he had to agree to some specific conditions, but in the end, Malcolm persuaded Jim to send him some of the experimental "Weyhauser Drug."

"You're the doctor," Jim laughed. "But I want a full report on your results."

CHAPTER 33

David was waiting in the driveway for Rhonda when she got home. She pulled the car past him into the garage and got out amidst the exhaust fumes. Coughing, she barely glanced at him when he walked in.

"What are you doing here?" she asked.

He followed her through the door that led from the garage to the kitchen. It was a white, spacious room in a white, spacious mansion. The note on the counter said that her parents were out for the evening.

Rhonda went to the refrigerator and pulled out a Coke. She didn't offer one to David. "Are you happy now that you have Sarah back?" she asked in a tone full of venom.

"I don't have her back," he replied. "I don't think *anyone* has her back—at least, not the Sarah we knew. The amnesia's for real."

Rhonda took another drink. "It doesn't matter. Now that Calvin knows she's seen you again, she'll have more than amnesia to deal with."

"How does Calvin know I saw her?"

She slid into a kitchen chair and dropped her soda can onto the table with a thud. "He's been following her. He saw you at the diner."

"So? What'll he do?" David asked.

Rhonda seethed. "You're an idiot. Calvin knew about you and Sarah long before you thought he did."

"Where are you getting all this information about Calvin?" David demanded. "How did he know?"

"Because I told him," Rhonda answered. "I was sick of stand-ing by while you two played lovebirds."

David was aghast. "Why would you tell Calvin?"

"You're really blind, aren't you? You just don't see the obvi-ous."

David strode forward and grabbed the drink from Rhonda's

hand. He turned her by the shoulders and looked straight at her. "What are you up to?" he growled. "What kind of game are you playing?"

She looked up at him, her eyes thin lines of disgust. "Get out of here."

David persisted, "Why did you tell Sarah that we used to go out?"

"I suppose you told her we didn't. Is that how you console your poor male ego, by denying there was anything between us, just because I dumped you?" She laughed derisively.

"Dumped me?" David asked. "How could you dump me when we weren't seeing each other? What are you trying to pull?"

Rhonda turned away from him and didn't answer.

"If this is another one of your schemes, it won't work!" David shouted. "You and Calvin won't stop us from being together if that's what we want to do."

Rhonda laughed again. "Did you really think Calvin was going to sit back and let Sarah meet you at the river that night—or *any* night? He'd kill her first."

CHAPTER 34

Malcolm and Jeff arrived at Elizabeth's house just as the sun threw its remaining orange over the walls and garden. At the front door, Jeff stopped.

"Are you sure this is all right?" he asked.

Malcolm opened the unlocked door. "Uh-huh. I explained to the Fordes that I wanted to test a theory about what happened to Elizabeth that night and that I needed to see her bathroom. They said they'd leave the door open for me when they went to the hospital."

They crossed through the cool foyer. Bookcases full of disheveled books, middle-eastern tapestries on the walls, and a large grandfather's clock made the place look like a set from a Sherlock Holmes movie.

"That's all you said, and they said okay?"

Malcolm looked at his nephew indignantly. "They trust me."

"*I* wouldn't," Jeff said as they headed up the stairs. "What theory? And what's that black bag for? How is this supposed to help Elizabeth?"

"You'll see."

"But—"

"Do you want to save Elizabeth or not?"

They walked on silently. At the top of the stairs, they turned left to go to Elizabeth's room. Jeff glanced around uneasily. He felt sneaky, as if they were invading her privacy.

The room itself unsettled him. Not that anything was wrong. On the contrary, it was *too* right; it was Elizabeth all over. He paused to take it in. The decorations, the posters, the knickknacks, the books at odd angles, the photos haphazardly scattered on the dresser and night stand were like her fingerprints on a canvas. He breathed in. The room smelled of her. He felt a pang in his chest. He missed her in the deepest part of his soul. If he could get her back, things would be different. No more "just friends" stuff. He wanted her for keeps.

Uncle Malcolm wandered into the bathroom. His voice echoed as he called out, "In here, Jeff."

Still unsure of his uncle's intentions, Jeff walked in and looked around.

"Sit down," Malcolm said as he gestured to the covered toilet. Jeff obeyed. "I'm going to explain what I want to do."

Jeff watched him expectantly.

Uncle Malcolm smiled awkwardly. "We're going to try to save Elizabeth by going to the alternative time to get her," he announced.

Jeff sat, openmouthed. "I don't understand," he eventually said.

Uncle Malcolm knelt next to the black bag, opened it, and pulled out two vials of a clear liquid and a hypodermic syringe. "If my theory is right, she's in great danger. You said so yourself."

"But we were just talking," Jeff began. "We were just, you know, playing a guessing game."

"Maybe *you* were talking and playing games. But I believe Elizabeth is stuck in an alternative time, and she may be in a life-threatening situation."

Jeff fidgeted nervously. "Then what—I mean, how—I mean—"

"This is a drug Dr. Weyhauser gave me. It's perfectly legal. Call it a dream drug, for lack of a better name. I think the 'Weyhauser Drug' sounds cumbersome, don't you?"

Jeff squirmed on the toilet lid. "Forget about the name of the drug, Uncle Malcolm. Could we go back to the part about going to an alternative time?"

"If my theory is right—and I'm convinced it is—and if this drug works as it should—and I'm not convinced it will—the part of the brain that establishes a dream-state or a state of *dèjá vu* will be stimulated. I think it's a bridge that leads to an alternative time." Malcolm plunged the needle into the top of the first vial and drew some of the clear liquid out. He then held the syringe up and primed the needle with a quick squirt.

Jeff gulped. "But . . . what if there are a whole bunch of alternative times?"

Malcolm's nose twitched. "That's one of the risks."

"One of them."

"There are others," he said in a matter-of-fact tone. "For one thing, the drug may fail completely. But, apart from a slight headache and a profound sense of disappointment, that's the least of our concerns."

"What else?"

He leaned against the tub and gave Jeff his full attention. "There may not be an 'alternative twin' to switch with. In which case, I don't have a clue about how to help Elizabeth."

"Uh-huh. And?"

"I'm not sure what will become of the alternative twin if he or she comes to our time," Malcolm said.

"Okay," Jeff said numbly. "Anything else?"

Malcolm nodded. "This is the biggest stickler of them all. I don't know how to get back." He knelt next to the black bag again and pulled out a cotton swab and alcohol. He rolled up the sleeve on his right arm and dabbed at the exposed skin.

"Wait a minute," Jeff said. "*You're* not going."

"Of course I am. But I need you to stay close by in case something goes wrong. He looked around the bathroom. "I think this is the best place to try it. I believe Elizabeth was in the bath when she crossed over."

"You can't go."

"Why not?"

"Because . . . I should go."

Uncle Malcolm chuckled. "Go where? You don't believe any of this nonsense."

Jeff leaned forward. "I don't know if I believe it or not, but I'll take the chance if it'll get me to Elizabeth."

"But, Jeff—"

"Look, it's more important for you to be here if something goes wrong. You can explain it to Sheriff Hounslow better than I can."

"Good point," he said, after thinking about it for a minute. He tugged at his ear. "But what if I can't get you back?"

Jeff set his jaw resolutely. "It doesn't matter. I love her, Uncle Malcolm, and I don't want to be here if she's not with me."

"Awwww . . . " Uncle Malcolm smiled.

Jeff blushed. "Hurry up before I change my mind."

"Okay." Uncle Malcolm reached down into the black bag again and brought out a micro-cassette recorder and tape. "For the record."

They looked at each other silently for a moment.

"God be with you," Uncle Malcolm said.

"He'd better be with us both," Jeff whispered.

Uncle Malcolm prepared Jeff's arm and injected the drug.

CHAPTER 35

Calvin's face was purple with rage. He shouted at Elizabeth, but his words were unintelligible. The name "David" was all she could pick out of the barrage.

They'd gone beyond the point of no return this time, she knew. There would be no manipulating him out of this mood. For the first time, she wished his parents were home. She didn't feel safe.

"I don't understand you!" he shouted, pacing around her room. "We could start all over again. We could make it work this time!"

"Make what work?" Elizabeth asked. "I don't know you. I don't even know *me!* How am I supposed to know what'll work? Why are you so mad?"

"Why did you lie to me?" he demanded. "Why did you meet him like that—sneaking around, making a spectacle of yourself—"

"What?"

"I saw you in the cafe! It was disgusting!" he shouted.

"You were spying on me?"

"I was following you for your own good!" he replied. "You're vulnerable right now. You need to be protected. You don't know what David's like. You don't remember."

"What else don't I remember, Calvin? Tell me what else happened the night I ran away!" Elizabeth challenged him. "Is there something *you* don't want me to know? Maybe you don't want me to remember!"

He roared at the ceiling and turned away. "You're driving me crazy!"

Elizabeth considered rushing out the door to escape. She calculated her odds and realized that he could outrun her. He leaned against the wall with his back to her, his shoulders hunched. The silence worried her.

"It was perfect. We could have started all over again," he said in a half-whisper. His voice got louder, and he spun around to face her. "I won't lose you again. Do you hear me? I won't lose you again."

Elizabeth reached her limit. "Listen to me, Calvin," she said. "I'm not going to play this game. I'm not Sarah, and I'll never be Sarah. Go ahead and have me committed if you want, but Sarah is gone. I'm Elizabeth!"

Calvin's face went ashen. "No," he said, stepping toward her. He reached out and grabbed her arm. "Is that who David wants you to be? Is this his idea?"

"David doesn't have anything to do with this," she started to say, but Calvin was beyond listening.

"Where are you going to meet him—down at the river again?" he yelled, tightening his grip.

"No," she gasped. "I'm not meeting David anywhere. Now let go of me!"

He pulled her closer. "You're not leaving me for David," he said. "I won't let you!"

She wrenched her arm free and made a move for the door, but Calvin seized her by the shoulder and spun her around. She lost her balance, crashing to the floor with a breathtaking thump as he moved toward her, his fists raised.

CHAPTER 36

At first Jeff didn't feel any different. Just a slight pinprick where the needle had been. Then he felt warm, as if someone had wrapped a blanket fresh from the dryer around him. Then Uncle Malcolm tilted a little to one side, then the other, then faded from view completely. Jeff thought his head had fallen forward, but he couldn't be sure. Darkness prevailed for a moment, and he felt completely at peace.

"Jeff?" Uncle Malcolm called out. But his voice was coming from the furthest point down a long tunnel.

Is this what it's like to be hypnotized? Jeff wondered. *Or dead?*

"Do you see anything?"

"No," Jeff answered. But he had spoken too soon. A flash of lightning penetrated the darkness, and Jeff was running. He was running harder than he'd ever run in his life. His heart raced. He was panicked.

"What's wrong, Jeff?" Uncle Malcolm's voice asked. "Why are you breathing so hard?"

"I'm running up to a house," Jeff said. "This house. I'm running up the driveway."

"What do you see?" Uncle Malcolm persisted.

"The front porch . . . up the stairs . . . I'm pushing through the front door. It's different inside . . . it's not this house . . . the front hall is different . . . I don't care . . . I have to get to her . . . I have to find her . . . what was that?"

It was a scream—and it sounded like Elizabeth.

"Tell me! Tell me!" Uncle Malcolm said.

Jeff gasped from his running. "To the second floor . . . my side hurts . . . Elizabeth's bedroom, the door is closed . . . I throw it open . . . Hey!"

He saw a boy he didn't recognize, standing over someone on the floor. The stranger spun around to face him.

"Wait!" Jeff cried out.

"What do you see?" Uncle Malcolm demanded.

It was Elizabeth on the floor—the floor of this room! Frenzied, Jeff opened his mouth to call out.

Everything went dark.

He woke up on Elizabeth's bed. Uncle Malcolm was standing over him with his brow furrowed from distress.

"Are you all right?" he asked.

Groggy, Jeff tried to sit up, but couldn't.

"Stay still," Uncle Malcolm said. "You've only been out for a minute. Boy, I was worried about you."

"I saw her!" Jeff croaked through a thick, pasty mouth. "It wasn't my imagination! It was real! I saw her! Give me another shot, Uncle Malcolm. I've got to get back to her. She's in trouble!"

CHAPTER 37

"Hey!" David yelled, then leapt on Calvin. They both crashed to the floor.

Elizabeth scrambled away, trying to keep from being crushed by the two of them as they rolled around, panting and heaving, throwing fists that hit nothing but carpet.

She couldn't figure out what had happened. One minute, Calvin was coming at her as though he might kill her. The next minute, David was rushing through the door and leaping on Calvin like a leopard.

Bracing herself against the closet, she clumsily got to her feet and tried to catch her breath.

David was no match for Calvin, and soon he was on the bottom being pummeled by Calvin's wild punches. Elizabeth screamed at them to stop. She rushed to pull Calvin off, but he swung back and hit her with the full force of his arm. It sent her into the bookshelf and knocked the wind out of her. She slumped to the ground, her breath a wheezing wind in her ears.

Then David and Calvin were both on their feet, locked in a strained, tortured embrace. Calvin pushed hard to his left, hoping David would lose his balance. It worked. Their legs tangled, and they lurched like a drunken spider into the night stand. The recently repaired lamp crashed down with a brilliant pop of its bulb. Then they were on the floor. Again, Calvin was on top. His hands were around David's throat.

He's going to kill him! Elizabeth's mind screamed. But the image she saw wasn't the scene in front of her, but a monster trying to kill Jeff. Clutching her side, she got to her feet and grabbed a heavy bookend shaped like a lion. Without grace or skill, she swung it and clobbered Calvin on the side of the head.

He collapsed to the floor, moaning.

Elizabeth's legs buckled, and she fell to her knees. She saw David struggling to stand; he sidestepped Calvin to get to her.

Grabbing both of her arms, he pulled her to her feet. "When he gets up, he'll be like a mad rhinoceros," he said in a raspy voice.

Without thinking, Elizabeth let him lead her out of the house.

CHAPTER 38

"Uncle Malcolm! You have to listen to me!"

Uncle Malcolm was muttering, lost in his own thoughts as he paced the room. "I have to think. Did you really make it through, or did you imagine it? What did you see? What did it mean?"

Jeff sat up on the bed impatiently, the effort nearly causing him to throw up. "I told you what I saw. I have to—"

"Yes, yes! What you saw!" Uncle Malcolm said without hearing Jeff. "If you saw something, it may have been through your *twin's* eyes. That must be it! And if you saw Elizabeth, then it means the two of you were together. Maybe she's in safe hands."

"No! She *isn't* safe!" Jeff cried out. "She's in trouble. I have to go back to help her!"

"That first injection went so quickly." Uncle Malcolm shook his head, then mused, "Obviously, I didn't give you a large enough dose. I wanted to be careful."

"I have to save Elizabeth!" Jeff pleaded. "Somebody was hurting her. You have to give me another shot! *Please!* You don't know what I saw or what I felt! She's in danger!"

Uncle Malcolm stared at Jeff, then he made up his mind. He disappeared into the bathroom and returned a moment later with the needle. "We'll try the full dose. That should give you more time there."

He injected another dose into Jeff.

Jeff stretched out across the bed. Uncle Malcolm watched him carefully. Shortly, Jeff's breathing took on the regular rhythm of sleep—a deep sleep that couldn't be penetrated by Uncle Malcolm's repeated calls. All of his vital signs were normal, so Malcolm decided to wait.

A anxious half hour passed.

Suddenly Jeff moved, tossing and turning as if he were having a nightmare. Then he called out "No!" at the top of his voice.

Then he grabbed his head and screamed in great pain.

CHAPTER 39

David drove his car without speaking to Elizabeth. He occasionally reached up to rub his throat.

They turned onto Church Road. In the Fawlt Line Elizabeth knew, it was a dirt track that led to the river. In Sarah's Fawlt Line, it was a nicely paved street with modern lighted signs giving directions to the Old Sawmill, a new development.

Within a mile, they turned right into an empty parking lot. Elizabeth could see the half-finished complex of condominiums. Even in her numb frame of mind, she was amazed at the contrast with the place she knew.

"What is all this?" she asked. "Where's the mill?"

David swung the car into a parking space close to a trailer labeled headquarters for the GWR Construction Company. "The *real* Old Sawmill is over there," he said, his voice still raspy. He pointed off to the left, toward the river, where a remnant of the old sawmill sat against a newer building. It had been restored and turned into the main office for the development. "There's a complex of condominiums going in here. My father is the real estate developer in charge of the project."

"What are we doing here?" Elizabeth asked.

David held up a key. "This'll get us into the office. There's a model condo inside. I figure it's the safest place until Calvin calms down."

"But he knows about it. He knows I was supposed to meet you at the river that night."

"Unless you told him before your amnesia, Calvin can't know where on the river." David opened his door and got out.

"Won't someone call the police on us?" Elizabeth asked as she opened the door and slid out onto the pavement.

David joined her at the door and put his hand gently through her arm. "There's nobody here. My dad's company is suing the contractor for breach of contract. The place has been empty for nearly two weeks. You don't recognize it?"

"No," Elizabeth said. They walked to the office, and David let them in.

"This is where you were supposed to meet me the night you lost your memory. I haven't been back since." He turned on a light, and Elizabeth flinched from the sudden brightness. "I hope they haven't dismantled the room. Follow me."

He guided her past the pristine modular furniture of gray and white and the framed artist's renderings of the complex. He pushed open a wood-paneled door and flipped another light switch. "Ah," he exclaimed.

Elizabeth found herself standing in a picturesque model apartment that could be featured in the best home-decorating magazines. *It's perfect*, she thought as she ran her finger over the cherrywood table that nicely complemented the sofa and the Chippendale chair with ottoman, all carefully arranged atop a Serapi-design rug. The colors were a mixture of rose and carnation-yellow in varying shades. The room exuded warmth and comfort.

"Not bad, huh?" David said. He stood near a large fireplace on the far wall, examining his throat in the gold-crested mirror above the mantel.

Elizabeth was horrified to see in the light how bruised his neck was. "Oh, David," she said and walked over to him. "I'm sorry." Their eyes met in the reflection in the mirror. "Thank you for saving me."

He smiled. "Don't mention it."

"I'm a mess," Elizabeth said to her reflection. Her hair was tangled, and her eyes looked tired and puffy.

"I didn't know Calvin had it in him. I never thought of him as the violent type," he said.

Elizabeth was surprised by the comment. Somewhere she had gotten the impression that everyone who knew Calvin knew he "had it in him."

"He has a bad temper," she explained. "A jealous streak. But I didn't think he'd go this far. What am I going to do? I can't go back." Wearily she put her face in her hands. "I can't go anywhere."

David put his arm around her and pulled her close. "Poor Sarah. We'll figure something out."

"David . . . I'm not Sarah," she whispered.

He smiled indulgently. "Whoever you are, then. We'll work it out." He guided her toward another door and turned on another light. "I think the best thing for you to do at the moment is to get some rest."

They stepped into an immaculately decorated bedroom with a four-poster bed and another fireplace. He led her to the foot of the bed, where she sat down.

"David, I'm confused," she confessed.

"About what?"

"The night I—I mean, *Sarah*—was supposed to meet you here. You said she didn't show up."

"That's right."

"But—why *didn't* she show up?"

David chuckled scornfully. "I've tortured myself with that question."

"But where did she go? Somebody must've seen her after she left Calvin's house. I can't believe she just walked around alone all that time."

David put a hand on her shoulder. "So you're playing detective to find out what happened to you?"

Elizabeth blushed.

"I think it's a mystery we'll never solve, unless you get your memory back. Which won't happen as long as you keep insisting that you're Elizabeth and not Sarah. Sarah's memory can't come back if she doesn't exist."

It was a rebuke, but Elizabeth pressed on. "Calvin said I was gone for two hours—supposedly to meet you. Then Rhonda kept dropping hints that I *did* meet you here."

"So who are you going to believe?" David asked as he stepped away from her.

"I don't know," Elizabeth said honestly. "None of it makes any sense. You're positive I didn't come here?"

"Positive," David said, then went into the bathroom. "I'm going to wash up."

"What happened in those two hours?" she asked the empty room. *I'm going to find out,* she promised herself. *I'm going to know the truth, and maybe it'll set me free.* She fell back onto the bed, stretched luxuriously, and rolled onto her side. The movement hurt her shoulder, and as she moved onto her back, her eye caught something sitting between the dresser and the wall. It was a purse.

Her first thought was that a saleswoman must have left it behind. Her second thought was that maybe David had invited *other* girls back to this model apartment. Her third thought was that she should see whose it was.

She glanced in the direction of the bathroom, where she could hear water running. Then she crept over to the dresser, stooped down, and picked up the purse. Returning to the edge of the bed, she sat down with her back to the bathroom door and the purse cradled in her lap.

She opened the clasp at the top and sneaked a peek inside. It was stuffed with tissues, wrappers, receipts, a makeup bag, and a wallet. Elizabeth pulled out the wallet and opened it. Several cards fell out. Hastily grabbing them up, she saw that the top card was an identification card for Fawlt Line High School.

Sarah, with heavy makeup and a jaded smile, looked up at Elizabeth.

Elizabeth stifled her surprise. *Sarah's purse? Then . . . she did meet David here that night. . . . Then . . . why had he lied to her?*

"Find something?" David asked from the foot of the bed.

CHAPTER 40

Startled, Elizabeth whirled around and dropped the purse. Its contents spilled onto the floor.

David chuckled as he toweled his face. "I didn't mean to scare you."

"David," Elizabeth said, "this is Sarah's purse. I found it next to the dresser. It's been lost since the night I lost my memory."

David looked stunned for a moment, then he gave a sigh of defeat. "Okay, it's true. You *did* come here that night."

"So why did you lie to me?"

David looked directly at her. "Because . . . I didn't want you to remember why you came. I thought maybe things could be different if you didn't remember."

That was just what Calvin said. It was his excuse to give them a new start. "What's going on here?" Elizabeth demanded furiously. "It's as if nobody really wants me to remember that night! Why did I come here? To run off with you?"

David dropped his eyes to the floor. "You came to say that you never wanted to see me again."

"Wait a minute. I didn't leave Calvin to run off with you? I left Calvin to come here and say that I was leaving you, too?"

David nodded. "You said you were going to take your parents' money, leave town, and start a new life somewhere else. You said you couldn't stand this place without your parents anymore. You needed to get away."

It took a few seconds for Elizabeth to digest this new bit of information. "Then what?" she asked.

"That's all. Nothing else happened, honest. I got mad and left, you stayed here. Until now, I didn't know you'd left your purse behind."

"Why should I believe you?"

"It's true," he answered.

A door slammed in the front part of the office.

"Calvin. He knew!" Elizabeth gasped.

"Get back," David whispered. He moved quickly toward the fireplace and reached for the poker.

Rhonda stalked into the room. "I am so sick of both of you," she announced. "Do you have any idea the mess you make wherever you go? You're nothing but trouble."

She sneered at David. "You thought you could turn on the charm, and I'd fall at your feet the way she did." She gestured toward Elizabeth. "But there was somebody better than you. He made you look like a fool."

"I don't know what's going on here, but maybe we'd better go," Elizabeth suggested.

David nodded, but Rhonda was between them and the door, and she wasn't about to move.

"I hated the way you hurt him. The way you took him for granted," she continued.

Elizabeth realized that Rhonda was talking to her now. "The way I took who for granted? What are you talking about?"

"Calvin, you idiot," Rhonda snarled. She stepped forward, closing the gap between them. "You still don't get it. You're so selfish. But he put up with it. I don't know how he can stand you."

Elizabeth was stunned. The characters in this bizarre little play kept shifting and changing in front of her eyes. Sarah tried to break up with both Calvin and David? Rhonda wanted Calvin? What was left? "You can have him," Elizabeth said. "I don't want him."

Rhonda laughed bitterly. "A wave of your precious hand, and he's mine? It's not that easy."

"Rhonda—" David began.

"Calvin wouldn't listen to me," she spit back. "I thought he would after he saw you two at the cafe. I thought he'd see that Sarah was the same old Sarah, whether she had amnesia or not. She's the same liar she always was."

David moved toward her, speaking gently. "Listen, Rhonda. Maybe we could talk about all this in the morning, when we're thinking more clearly. Sarah's had—"

But Rhonda was beyond reason. With a vicious motion, she slapped him across the face, then rushed past him and grabbed for the poker, which was lying on the floor where he'd dropped it.

"Stop her!" Elizabeth cried out.

David pivoted toward Rhonda in time to deflect the first blow with one arm. With the other he reached to grab the poker, missed, and stumbled. Rhonda swung the poker around and caught him solidly on the side of the head.

Elizabeth screamed as David cried out, clutched his head, and collapsed onto the bed.

CHAPTER 41

Jeff's scream made Uncle Malcolm's skin crawl.

Enough is enough, he thought. *I never should have given him that second shot.*

Jeff suddenly relaxed—no, slumped—into the bed. Uncle Malcolm moved closer. Jeff had gone pale, his hair was matted with sweat. His pulse was faint.

Something had gone wrong, Malcolm knew. Jim hadn't mentioned anyone ever experiencing side effects like these. He sped to the night stand and grabbed the phone to call an ambulance.

He had just put the receiver to his mouth when he glanced back toward Jeff. The phone slipped from his hand.

Jeff was gone.

CHAPTER 42

Elizabeth rushed to David. It seemed to her as if Jeff himself had been struck down.

Rhonda looked panicked. "Oh no oh no oh no," she muttered.

Elizabeth cradled David's bleeding head with one hand and pressed the bed cover against it with the other. "Call an ambulance!" she shouted, but Rhonda didn't move.

"Now!" Elizabeth commanded and turned her attention to David.

"You were always a tramp," Rhonda said to Elizabeth. She raised the poker again.

From the corner of her eye, Elizabeth saw the movement and threw herself at Rhonda. It was a clean tackle that caught Rhonda by surprise and sent the poker clattering onto the hearth. They crashed into the wall, then to the floor. Rhonda, who was in far better shape than Elizabeth, quickly escaped her grip and leapt to her feet. Suddenly she froze, her expression one of stunned horror. Putting her hand to her mouth, she staggered back against the fireplace.

Elizabeth struggled to her feet and followed Rhonda's gaze to the bed.

David had disappeared.

CHAPTER 43

Jeff opened his eyes and looked around. The room was dark. He sat up on the bed and felt a strange sensation in the pit of his stomach. Something was different. "Uncle Malcolm?" he whispered.

No answer.

He slowly swung his legs off the bed and tried to stand. It wasn't easy. He scanned the room, bewildered by what he saw.

It was Elizabeth's room, all right, but small details caught his attention: a picture was in a different place, the bedspread had changed, a poster was missing from the closet door.

He held his swimming head and stepped into the hall. On the left he saw a light coming from the spare room. *Maybe Uncle Malcolm decided to rest,* he thought, not certain what time it was or how long he'd been asleep.

He used the wall to steady himself and bumped into a table that wasn't there before. The potted plant and pictures shook. He looked down and saw some photos of Elizabeth—with someone Jeff had never seen before.

I'm dreaming, he said to himself.

Then he noticed the drops on the carpet. He knelt and put the tip of his finger into one. Fresh blood. His heart skipped a beat as he sprinted for the light. "Elizabeth?" he cried out.

He rounded the corner and went into the room. Suddenly, he was grabbed from behind and wrestled into a half-nelson.

Jeff struggled wildly, but to no avail. His attacker was the guy he'd seen before, standing over Elizabeth in her room.

"Let me go!" he shouted.

The boy snickered and spoke into Jeff's ear, his tone as casual as if the two of them were having a chat over the breakfast table. "What's wrong with you? Why did you come back?"

"I don't know what—"

The boy quickly adjusted his hold so that it was no longer a half-nelson, but a stranglehold. It closed off Jeff's windpipe. "Why aren't you with Sarah?"

"Who?" Jeff croaked as he clawed at his attacker's arms.

"You've done enough damage. We had a second chance, but you couldn't stay away, could you?"

Jeff struggled against the viselike grip. He kicked and clawed, then black spots appeared and he sank down as dead weight.

CHAPTER 44

At the Old Sawmill in Fawlt Line, David woke up on an old threadbare mattress that had been shoved into a corner. Its springs poked through the fabric, and it was covered with sawdust. His head was spinning from the blow Rhonda had given him. Gingerly he touched a finger to a spot just above his right ear. Through hair that was thick with blood, he could feel the gash.

"Let me help you," someone said.

David looked through misty eyes. A tall, slender man with an ageless face and gold-white hair reached for him. David felt too weak to resist. *What happened? Where is Sarah? Where is Rhonda? Where is the condo? Where on earth am I?*

The stranger put his arms around David and helped him to his feet. "Would it mean anything if I called you Jeff?" he asked politely as he guided David to the door.

David slowly shook his head.

"I didn't think so," the stranger said with an undeniable sound of pleasure in his voice.

"Where am I?" David asked as they stepped into the clear night.

"The Old Sawmill," Malcolm Dubbs answered. "I just knew it was part of the equation somehow."

"Equation?"

Malcolm didn't hear him. "I'd wager that the hospital plays into it, too."

"I don't understand," David said.

Malcolm smiled. "I don't expect you to. I'll explain it at the hospital, if there's time."

"The hospital?"

"You need to have your head looked at," Malcolm answered. "And I want to hear everything you can tell me about a girl in a coma."

CHAPTER 45

Again Jeff opened his eyes and looked around. But this time he did so just as the lid of a car trunk slammed shut above him. He threw his arm upward, but it was too late. "Hey!" he cried weakly.

"Shut up," a muffled voice growled from the other side. He heard his abductor get into the car, close the door, and start the motor.

As they drove, Jeff could hear rock music from the car radio blaring and thumping through the rear speakers. He felt around in the dark, hoping to find something that would help him break out.

They drove onward. The combination of heat, fumes, and sweat was dizzying to Jeff. He felt as if he were on the inside of a clothes dryer as they bounced along. He heard water splashing the undercarriage.

Under the trunk carpet he found a tire jack. He wedged the jack into the trunk lock, hoping to break it from the inside.

The car stopped, and Jeff heard the driver get out. He got a firm hold on the jack. *If this guy opens up the trunk, I'm gonna pay him back big time.*

There was a pounding on the trunk lid. "Anybody home?" a voice asked.

Jeff didn't answer.

"Good," said the voice. Jeff listened closely. The guy walked off.

Jeff waited, then put all his effort into breaking the lock. It wouldn't yield. His sweaty hands slipped, and finally he collapsed, exhausted.

His mind raced. What could he do except conquer the lock? He railed against it one last time with all his power, pushing, pulling, yanking, straining.

No good.

Frustrated, he cried out in a long, painful howl. "Let me out of heeeeerrrreee!"

Just then, the latch clicked and the trunk opened.

CHAPTER 46

Rhonda's wide eyes darted around the model condominium. Sure that David was going to attack her from somewhere, she held the poker like a sword to ward him off.

Elizabeth stood frozen where she was, not sure what to think about David's sudden disappearance. Suddenly she realized that she had a clear passage to the door. "Run, David!" she screamed and dashed away.

She raced from the bedroom, through the living room and the office, and out the front door into the star-filled night. *Free*, she thought. *I'm free.*

"Whoa!" a voice called out. Strong hands grabbed her and yanked her entire body off the ground and backward into even stronger arms and a brick wall of a chest.

She knew who it was.

"Calvin!" she gasped. "Help me!"

Still holding her arm, Calvin let go so she could turn and face him. "It'll be all right," he said soothingly.

Everyone has gone nuts, she thought and jerked her arm away to escape.

"Huh-uh," he said, catching her wrist and twisting it.

Rhonda, haggard and panicked, appeared in the doorway, still clutching the poker. "What are we going to do with her?" Rhonda shouted. "She'll go to the police! It's a mess! This whole thing has turned into another mess!"

Calvin looked sadly at Elizabeth. "Why didn't you stay away? Why did you have to come back if you weren't going to make it work? Why didn't you just stay dead?"

"Stay *dead*?" Elizabeth said. "When did you think I was dead?"

"You *were* dead," Calvin lamented, "when I put you in the river."

Instantly, the image returned. Rough hands grabbing her, hard fingers wrapping around her throat, pressing tight, pushing her under filthy brown water.

"I figured it was better than to lose you to David," he said.

At last she understood. All the pieces snapped into place.

"No!" Elizabeth screamed and raked her clawed fingers across Calvin's face as she wrenched her wrist away from him. Rhonda raised the poker, but Elizabeth spun wildly, clasping her hands together as though she was about to hit a volleyball—but connecting with Rhonda's jaw instead. She didn't wait to see the effect, but stumbled into the woods and raced toward the river.

But the river wasn't where it should have been. Instead, Elizabeth cleared the woods to find herself running along a makeshift dock, obviously created for the delivery of supplies to the construction crew. She reached a wooden rail at the end of it, stopping for a moment to decide whether or not to jump over and risk the ten-foot fall into the water.

That moment of indecision was all Calvin needed. He caught her by the hair and pulled her back. His free hand clenched her throat.

"I thought we had a second chance, but you spoiled it again," he said mournfully. Elizabeth saw the tears on his cheeks. He tightened his grip around her throat.

Pounding her fists against his chest, she tried to scream. Nothing came out.

This is it. This is the end of what started in the bathtub. Why didn't I just die then?

She swam in and out of consciousness. Any power in her body faded as her arms flapped against Calvin like two strips of cloth in the wind.

Suddenly they heard a scream, but it was quickly choked off.

Calvin turned away from Elizabeth to look. With her remaining strength, she lashed at him. It freed her from his grip, but only for a second. He backhanded her, knocking her against the rail. Instantly, he had her by the throat again. He pressed her against the railing and leaned all his weight into this final attack. She couldn't breathe. Black spots splashed on her eyes like drops of oil.

There was a loud crack as the railing gave way. They both fell over the side of the dock. Elizabeth expected—even waited for—their splash into the cold river, but instead, they landed side-by-side with a dull thud on a construction barge below. The wind was knocked out of her, and a sharp pain shot through her wrist. She wanted to scream, but only a wheezing sound came out. Calvin groaned, then rolled over and got to his feet. Elizabeth was completely disoriented. She tried to crawl away from him, sobbing as he reached out in time to catch her blouse. The cloth tore, but then he had her arm and dragged her toward him.

A dark figure rose up behind Calvin. "Behind you!" it called out, and Calvin turned. Like a batter swinging for a fast ball, the dark figure brought a two-by-four crashing against Calvin's head. There was nowhere for him to go but down.

Elizabeth lay back on the barge, barely conscious. She couldn't take any of it in. Above her, she thought she could see Rhonda on the dock. David was there too, restraining her.

Rhonda screamed and broke free, then scrambled down the flight of stairs connecting the dock to the barge. There she cradled Calvin in her arms.

David also descended to the barge as the dark figure moved toward Elizabeth. He knelt next to her, out of the shadows and into the glow from a light above. It was Crazy George.

"I told you something was gonna happen," he said proudly.

Then David knelt next to Crazy George, leaned closer, and pulled Elizabeth to his chest.

"David . . ." she whispered hoarsely.

"No, Bits," he replied. "It's Jeff."

CHAPTER 47

"Boy, when you run away, you really run away," Jeff said to Elizabeth. She was nestled in the four-poster bed in the Old Sawmill's model apartment, certain that she was in shock—or had slipped into yet another dream world.

"Jeff?" she whispered.

"Yeah?" He leaned over and gently touched her hair.

Tears formed in the corners of her eyes. "Is it really you?"

"It's me." He smiled.

Her head was swimming. "Jeff . . ."

"You need to rest until the ambulance gets here," Jeff said.

"Phone's out. I'll have to drive to a pay phone to get an ambulance and police," Crazy George announced as he entered the room.

"Where's what's-his-name?" Jeff asked.

Crazy George tipped his head toward the other room. "Calvin? On the sofa in the office. I whacked him pretty good. I'm gonna take him with me."

Jeff glanced warily at the office. "Is he going to—?"

"Behave himself?" Crazy George nodded. "He's like a whipped puppy. He'll be fine. It's the other one I'm worried about—the girl. She took off."

"Probably headed for the hills," Jeff said, then winced as his cuts and bruises came to life.

Crazy George frowned. "I'll call for help, then come right back. Okay? You'll be all right?"

Jeff nodded.

George's face suddenly brightened with a smile he'd obviously been restraining for a while. He looked around to make sure Calvin wasn't eavesdropping. "So, be honest now. You're from the other time, aren't you?"

"I guess I am. I mean, we are."

George clapped his hands together and laughed. "I knew it. I knew it."

"I guess somebody switched the channels," Elizabeth said weakly from the bed.

"I guess so."

Good old George, she thought. *He wasn't crazy after all.*

She looked at him a moment. It surprised her to suddenly be filled with a feeling of deep respect for him, that he could believe for so long in something he knew to be true, but that no one else believed. Her parents came to her mind—with their churchgoing and their "eternal perspective." She realized that they might be right after all. There was so much more to life than she knew. And it took this journey to prove it.

George smiled as if he knew what she was thinking.

"George, how did you know about tonight?" she asked.

He stepped toward the bed. "I told you something was going to happen, didn't I? I told you we had to stick together."

"I didn't do a very good job of sticking," Elizabeth said meekly.

"I know. So I kept my eye on you. I followed you to the Old Sawmill after you left the house with David. I waited for you, then got worried when that girl Rhonda and then what's-his-name Calvin showed up." He turned his gaze to Jeff. "I heard you banging around in the trunk. Fortunately Calvin's car has one of those jiggly flippers under the front seat, so I could let you out. 'Bout scared the wits out of me too. There you were in the trunk, when I had seen you go into the office with my own two eyes. Unless you were twins, I knew I was right."

"Hey," Calvin called from the other room. "Are we going, or are you going to let me bleed to death in here?"

George rolled his eyes. "I'm coming!" he called back. Then he turned to Jeff. "I have a million questions I want to ask you. I'll be back as fast as I can." He zipped up his jacket as he spoke.

It was an old leather bomber-style jacket that Jeff guessed was very expensive at one time. He glanced at the name stitched into the front, and his mouth fell open. But George was gone before he could say anything.

"Okay," Elizabeth began, trying to sit up in the bed. She winced and stayed where she was. "You have to tell me what happened. How did you get here? How did I get here? Are we in Fawlt Line? Am I still dreaming? What's going on?"

"I'll tell you if you close your eyes and try to sleep," Jeff said. "Think of it as a bedtime story."

She nodded and closed her eyes as Jeff tried to explain as much as he could about Uncle Malcolm's theory and alternate time.

Elizabeth couldn't believe it. She'd never believe it.

"Me either," Jeff said.

She told him a brief version of her story—her treatment for amnesia, Crazy George, and the mystery surrounding Sarah's "last night." She figured it was safe to say that on the night of the changeover, Calvin and possibly Rhonda had followed Sarah to the Old Sawmill condo, where they grabbed her after David left. Calvin, in a jealous rage, fought with Sarah, strangled her, and dropped her into the river. That's what she saw while she was in the tub. Her bath and Sarah's struggle took place at the exact same time.

Jeff shook his head. "What are the odds that all those coincidences could happen in just the right way so that—"

"Watch what you say about coincidences." Elizabeth smiled and shook her finger at him. "Mom and Dad say they're the secret workings of God." She closed her eyes and exhaled slowly, sleepily.

Jeff watched her. *I never want to take my eyes off her again,* he thought, and then, *What a sap I am.*

Suddenly he realized that she was looking back at him. "You were staring at me," she said groggily.

He moved closer. "Can't help it," he said.

They locked gazes. The words formed in both of their minds. *I love you,* they wanted to say.

He leaned over and kissed her. Then he put his hand over her eyes so she'd have to keep them closed. "Rest, Bits. We'll get out of here in no time at all."

"Out of where?" she asked from beneath his hand. "Are we going home?"

He didn't answer. Now wasn't the time to tell her that there was no going home. "Just rest," he said.

CHAPTER 48

David refused to believe anything Malcolm told him. He didn't go so far as to call Malcolm a liar or a lunatic, but his expression said as much. He wouldn't speak while a doctor in the emergency room stitched the gash on the side of his head. Finally, when the doctor insisted on knowing how the gash got there, he simply said he fell down.

Sheriff Hounslow and Mr. and Mrs. Forde were in Elizabeth's room at the hospital. When Malcolm appeared with the bandaged David, everyone greeted them as usual.

Hounslow was the first to notice David's bandage. "What happened to your head, Jeff?"

David stared at Sarah, still comatose in the bed, and said quietly, "No."

"What did you say?"

"I'm not Jeff," David said as he slowly moved to the side of the bed.

Hounslow looked at Malcolm. "What did he say?"

"I think we need to watch closely," Malcolm replied.

David knelt next to the bed. "Sarah, what did they do you to you?" He looked up at Malcolm with stricken eyes. "I don't understand. I must be losing my mind. How did she get like this? Did I black out? Did Calvin do this?"

Hounslow folded his arms irritably. "What's he talking about?"

"What did he call her?" Alan Forde asked.

"Sarah," David answered.

Jane Forde looked worried. "What's wrong with you, Jeff? That's Elizabeth."

"Elizabeth!" The name connected with him. He shook his head and staggered away from the bed. "No, it can't be true. That was *her* name, the *other* Sarah. But then who's *this*? Is she really—? No, it's impossible."

His face filled with panic, and he turned as if to run, but

Hounslow blocked the door. "Just what's going on here?"

Malcolm grabbed David's arm. "Come with me, David. There may be a way to fix this."

David looked helplessly at Malcolm.

"Let's find a room," Malcolm said.

The waiting room down the hall was the best they could do. Malcolm told David to sit down on the couch.

"You wanna let me in on this?" Hounslow said as he hovered restlessly. "I want some explanations."

"Later, Sheriff," Malcolm said. He pulled a syringe from the black leather bag.

"If you think this little trick is going to take Jeff off the suspect list, you have another think coming," Hounslow said.

"What're you going to do?" David asked Malcolm.

"This'll help you relax."

David sat up. "I don't want to relax. I want to think clearly. I want to wake up."

"Wake up?" Hounslow repeated.

"Maybe this will help you wake up," Malcolm said. He looked at David earnestly. "You have to trust me, David."

"Do I have a choice?"

"No."

David nodded. "Then do it."

Malcolm prepared David's arm, then injected the dream drug.

Hounslow shuffled nervously. "That's it. I'm getting a real doctor." He stormed off.

Back in Elizabeth/Sarah's room, Alan and Jane Forde quietly discussed Jeff's strange behavior. Alan was about to write it off as the result of stress, when Elizabeth suddenly began to thrash violently.

"Oh, no!" Jane cried out.

The girl's flailing arms threatened to pull out the IV tubes, and Alan leapt up to hold them down. "Get a nurse!" he barked at his wife.

Jane raced out of the room and into the hall, screaming for help as she ran.

CHAPTER 49

What's taking George so long? Jeff wondered as he dried his face with a towel. A loud bump came from the other room, and Jeff thought it was the door. *Right on cue.* He tossed the towel over a rack and opened the bathroom door.

What he saw was so unexpected that it took a second to sink in. A girl—the girl named Rhonda that he had grabbed on the dock—was on top of Elizabeth, pressing a pillow over her face. Elizabeth's pinned arms were thrashing under Rhonda's knees.

Jeff rushed forward and threw himself at the girl. His body slammed into hers, and they both rolled off the bed and onto the floor. Jeff's head hit against a dresser, fazing him long enough to allow her to get to her feet.

"You won't win this time," she announced. She grabbed a marble statuette, lifted it above her head, and threw it at Jeff's face.

He moved quickly to the right, and the marble hit the floor and fractured. He felt hard chips spray the side of his face. Reaching out, he grabbed her ankle and pulled with all his strength. She tripped, fell, then kicked at his hand. She scrambled for the fireplace, and he knew she was after the poker. *She's out of her mind*, he thought.

He jumped to his feet and was unnerved to see that the bed was empty. Elizabeth was gone.

"I won't be fooled again," Rhonda said. She had the poker in her hand now. The image gave Jeff a strange sense of *dèjá vu*. He knew he'd done this before.

She thrust the poker at Jeff, and he dodged it. Deftly she grasped it with both hands, spun her arms around, and swung the weapon with all her might. He dived toward the open door leading into the office. The poker smashed into a dresser. He skidded along the floor and hurried to his feet, but the force of his weight kept him off balance. Then he stumbled to the far wall and slammed down on the couch. The wooden armrest caught him in the ribs with a loud crack. A sharp pain shot through his body, and he cried out.

Rhonda sprinted from the bedroom into the office, her poker poised for a final blow. Just then George stepped through the door and grabbed her wrist, turning it sharply so the poker dropped to the floor. He brought the full force of his elbow against her face, knocking her against the desk and scattering papers and advertising booklets.

"Thanks," he said to her as blood poured from her nose. "You saved the police a lot of extra time hunting for you."

He glanced around the room to see who it was she was trying to hit with the poker. There was no one there.

CHAPTER 50

Jane Forde raced back to the hospital room with a nurse and Sheriff Hounslow in tow. In the doorway she suddenly stopped.

Alan Forde stood next to the bed. His face was whiter than any of the sheets. His mouth moved, but no words came out.

The hospital bed was empty.

In the waiting room, Malcolm stared at the empty couch where David had been sitting only a second before. He had hoped that if, by chance, a switch took place, it would bring Jeff to that same spot. Obviously, the process wasn't so predictable.

Think, Malcolm, think. He tugged at his ear. *Where are they? How can I find them?*

Hounslow rounded the corner into the waiting room. His face was flushed and his eyes wide and angry. "She's gone! He said she just disappeared right in front of his eyes! *What's going on here?*"

Malcolm smiled mischievously and shrugged. "We can search the hospital. But in the meantime, you might want to send a man to the Fordes' house to check Elizabeth's room." He snapped the black bag closed, then remembered where he had first found David. "Oh—and maybe we should check the Old Sawmill, too."

Hounslow glared at him.

The abandoned office at the Old Sawmill had a desk, a chair, and a visitor's sofa. Jeff woke up—if waking up was the right phrase—slung halfway off the sofa. He tried to stand, but the pain of a cracked rib stopped him. "Ouch!" he complained loudly.

"Hello?" came a voice from another part of the mill.

Clutching his side, Jeff struggled to his feet. As he opened the office door, he noticed an old yellowed calendar on the wall. "Hopwood's Sawmill," it said. He knew exactly where he was.

Elizabeth stood in the center of the mill's work area. Jeff stepped into view. "Jeff!" she cried out and ran to him.

"Wait, no!" he warned her as she tried to hug him. "I hurt myself."

She stepped back. "How did you get here?"

"I guess Rhonda and her Mad Poker chased me here somehow," he said. "How about you?"

"Rhonda and her Mad Pillow," Elizabeth replied, then gestured to an old mattress in the far corner of the shop. She smiled, then winced. Her cuts and bruises were still fresh. "Jeff, I'm afraid to ask, but . . . are we home?"

He put his arm around her, and together they walked to the door.

"Yeah, Bits," he answered. "You're finally home."

CHAPTER 51

"There's no place like home," Malcolm chuckled.

Hounslow adjusted his belt irritably. "What in the world is going on here? This doesn't make sense."

He looked across the emergency room ward. Elizabeth was in the midst of a tear-filled reunion with her parents.

"Well?" Hounslow asked.

"Ouch," Jeff said to the nurse who was taping up his damaged rib. "That hurt."

"Sorry," she said. "That's all we can do. You can put on your shirt now."

"I want a full explanation of what happened," Hounslow persisted. He turned to Jeff. "How did you get from the waiting room to the Old Sawmill?"

Jeff wasn't listening. He was watching Elizabeth. Somehow she knew it and looked back at him. She smiled and waved for him to join them. "Excuse me," he said. He walked over to her.

"Malcolm—" Hounslow began.

Malcolm sighed. "I'll explain it to you . . . but I don't think you'll believe me."

"Try me."

"Okay. But first you have to tell me if you believe in eternity."

Hounslow frowned. "Eternity? You mean, like going to church and things like that? Yeah, I guess I do. Sort of."

"That'll have to do, I suppose." Malcolm smiled wearily. "Let me begin by explaining a theory I have about time. . . ."

Malcolm was right. Hounslow didn't believe him.

CHAPTER 52

George hummed pleasantly to himself as he drilled the last screw into the hinge. It had needed tightening for a long time.

He heard animated talking from down the hall and looked expectantly in the direction of the sound. A wheelchair appeared from one of the rooms. In it was a girl named Sarah. She'd been in a coma for a few days, and was the talk of the hospital. Apparently she had just mysteriously appeared in one of the beds in the middle of the night.

She was being released from the hospital today and, by hospital rules, she had to go out in a wheelchair. She didn't seem to mind. A young man with wavy black hair and an open, friendly face was pushing it.

"Slow down, David," she said to the young man.

"*You* want me to slow down? Since when does Sarah Bishop want anything on wheels to go slow?"

"Since now." She smiled up at him.

He leaned down and kissed her as they wheeled past George. They saw him, but showed no sign that they recognized him.

No reason they should, George thought and put the drill down on his work cart. When he got around the corner, he found himself on the same elevator with them. They were laughing and talking happily. He hoped it would last. There were trials ahead, or so he had read in an article in the morning paper, and they'd both be part of them. Attempted murder, assault . . . Calvin and Rhonda were in deep trouble.

I wonder how it'll all turn out.

Oblivious to him, they got off at the lobby. George continued to the basement where he made his way to a locker. He opened it and took out a lunch pail. *I'll eat in the park today,* he decided. He grabbed his old bomber jacket and put it on. For a moment, he paused to touch the name stitched on the left breast. Sometimes the name made him sad, but today he felt okay about it. It wasn't just some name. It was a name with a history, with memories. He knew it now as surely as he knew anything. And even though people called him George, he knew that the stitched name was *his* name.

Charles Richards, it said.

It's okay, he thought and punched out at the time clock for lunch in the park. Maybe, for some reason, Sarah and David would go to the park, too. Maybe he'd get a chance to talk to them. Wouldn't that be a nice coincidence?

Here's what other readers are saying about Paul McCusker's Time Twists novels . . .

"This series is great. The plots are so exciting I could hardly put the books down."
—Erin D.

"The books are wonderful! I stayed up until five A.M. reading one because it was so exciting!"
—Katie S.

"Your novel made me think. It made me ask questions. You also painted a picture in my mind while I was reading."
—Natalie R.

"It was such an intriguing book I didn't even notice when I was turning the pages. The story has a good moral for kids.
—Philip B.

"The book was very adventurous. . . . When I get a good book like this one, I just can't put it down."
—Jacob A.

CHAPTER ▮ 1   Stranger in the Mist

A tall, gray old man stepped to the pinnacle of Glastonbury Tor, an unusual cone-like hill on which stood a tower named for a saint. In the wet English twilight, the wind whipped the old man's long gray hair and beard and his ragged brown monk's robe like a flag in a gale. The dark clouds above moved and gathered as if they thought him a curiosity worth investigating. Chalice Hill and Wearyall Hill waited in attendance nearby, their shoulders hunched like two old porters. The battered abbey beyond Chalice Hill listened in silence, unable to see from its skewered position.

The old man, a soloist before a strange orchestra, cast a sad eye to the green quilt littered with small houses and shops. They were an indifferent audience.

The old man prayed silently for a moment, then pulled an old curved horn from under his habit. He placed it to his lips and blew once, then twice, then a third time. The three muted blasts were caught by the wind and carried away.

The overture was finished, the program was just beginning.

"Look at that," Ben Hearn said to his wife, Kathryn. "It's crazy, I tell you. Crazy."

"What's crazy, Ben?" Kathryn suddenly asked, peering through the unusual fog.

"Didn't you see the sign for Malcolm Dubbs's village?"

Kathryn hadn't. But they were on one of the roads bordering the vast Dubbs estate, and she knew what sign her husband was talking about. It was the one that announced the construction of Malcolm Dubbs's Historical Village.

"I don't know what the town council was thinking when they agreed to it," Ben said. Malcolm was the most wealthy citizen of their little town of Fawlt Line. In fact, his family had been there for close to two centuries. Malcolm, a history buff, had designated a large portion of his property for the village.

Kathryn squinted at the fog ahead. "Don't you think you should slow down? It's getting thicker."

The truck engine whined as Ben heeded his wife. "You know what he's doing with the village, right? He's shipping in *buildings*. Brick by brick and stone by stone from all over the world. Have you ever heard of such a thing? A museum with a few trinkets and artifacts I could understand, but buildings?"

Kathryn smiled. "Malcolm always was obsessed with history. I remember when we were in school together—"

Ben wasn't listening. "Do you know what they've been working on for the past few weeks? Some kind of a ruin from England. A monastery or castle or cathedral, I don't know for sure."

"From England?" Kathryn asked, instantly lost in the romance of the idea. Then she grinned. "Did he have this fog shipped in too?"

Ben grunted, "I just don't understand Malcolm's fascination with something that's ruined. What's the point?"

Kathryn was about to answer—and would have—if a

man on horseback hadn't suddenly appeared on the road in front of them. The fog cleared just in time for Ben to see him, mutter an oath as he hit the brakes, and jerk the steering wheel to the right. The horse reared wildly, and the rider flew backward to the ground. Kathryn cried out as the truck skidded into a ditch on the side of the road and came to a gravel-spraying stop. Ben and Kathryn looked at each other shakily.

"You all right?" Ben asked.

Kathryn nodded.

"Of all the stupid things to do—" Ben growled and angrily pushed his door open. The angle of the truck threatened to spring it back on him. He pushed harder and held it in place as he crawled out. "Stay here," he said before the door slammed shut again.

Kathryn reached over and turned on the emergency flashers.

The on-and-off yellow light barely penetrated the fog that swirled around Ben's feet. He made his way cautiously down the road. "Fool," Ben muttered to himself, then called out. "Hello? Are you all right?"

The fog parted as if to show Ben the man lying on the side of the road.

"Oh no," Ben said, rushing forward. He crouched down next to the figure. Whoever it was seemed to be wrapped in a dark blanket. He was perfectly still. Even in the darkness, Ben could tell he was a bear of a man. His face was hidden in the fog and shadows.

"Hey," Ben said, hoping the man would stir. Ben looked him over for any sign of blood. Nothing was obvious around his head. But what could he expect to see in the darkness?

"Kathryn!" he shouted back toward the car. "Bring me the flashlight from the glove compartment!"

He peered closely at the shadowed form of the man as he heard Kathryn open her door. *What's the guy doing in a blanket? Why's he riding a horse so late in the evening? Why would anyone dash across a road thick with fog?* The crunch of his wife's shoes on the gravel came closer. The shaft of light from the flashlight bounced around eerily in the ever-moving fog.

Kathryn joined him and beamed the light at the stranger. He had long dark salt-and-peppery hair, beard, and mustache and a rugged, outdoorsy kind of face. Anywhere from forty to sixty years old, Ben figured. He wore a peaceful expression. He could've been sleeping.

"He's not dead, is he?" Kathryn asked, reacting in her own way to the peculiar serenity on the man's face.

"I don't think so." Ben reached down, separating the blanket to check the man's vital signs. The feel of the cloth told him it wasn't a blanket at all. As he pushed the fabric aside, he realized that it was a cape made of a thick coarse material, clasped at the neck by a dragon brooch. "What in the world—?"

Kathryn gasped.

They expected to see a shirt or a sweater or a coat of some sort. Instead the man wore a long vest with the symbol of a dragon stitched on the front, a gold belt, brown leggings, and soft leather footwear that looked more like slippers than shoes. The whole outfit reminded Ben of a costume in a Robin Hood movie. At the stranger's side was a sword in a sheath.

"Is it Halloween?" Kathryn asked.

Ben shook his head. "I think I'd better get the truck out of that ditch so you can go for help."

CHAPTER ▮ 1 ▮   Memory's Gate

What in the world am I doing here? Elizabeth Forde asked
herself as she followed Mrs. Kottler, a silver-haired woman,
down the main hallway of the Fawlt Line Retirement Center.

*Of all the things I could have spent the rest of my summer
doing, why this?* Yes, she had agreed to volunteer at the retirement center. She had even felt enthusiastic about the idea at
the time. But walking down the cold, clinical, pale green hallway with the smell of pine disinfectant in the air, Elizabeth
wondered if she had made a mistake.

She'd been swept along by Reverend Armstrong's pas-
sionate call to the young people of the church. He had exu-
berantly insisted that they get involved in the community.
They must be a generation of givers rather than takers, he
said. His words were powerful and persuasive, and before
she knew what she was doing she had joined a line of other
young people to sign up for volunteer service. Just a few
hours a day, three or four days a week, for a couple of weeks.
It hadn't sounded like much.

An old man, bent like a question-mark, stepped out of
his room and smiled toothlessly at her.

It's too much, she thought as they entered the recreation
room. *Let me out of here.*

A tall, handsome young man entered through a door at

the opposite end of the room. "Mrs. K., I was wondering—"

"Doug Hall, come meet Elizabeth Forde," Mrs. Kottler said, waving her arms as if she might create enough of a breeze to drag Doug over to them.

Doug strode across the room with a smile that showed off the deep dimples in his cheeks. *He's a movie star*, Elizabeth thought. His curly brown hair, perfectly formed face, large brown eyes, and a build that was enhanced, not hidden, by the white clinical coat made her certain. *He's a movie star playing a doctor*, she amended.

Doug reached her with an outstretched hand and said, "Well, my enjoyment of this place just increased by a hundred per cent."

She shook his hand and blushed. "Hi."

"Doug is our maintenance engineer," Mrs. Kottler explained.

Doug smiled again. "She means I'm the main janitor. But I'm more like a bouncer, in case these old madcap merrymakers get out of control with their wild partying and carousing."

Suddenly Elizabeth wondered how she appeared to Doug. How did she look in her freshly-issued white-and-pink clinic jacket—frumpy or professional? Had she taken pains with her makeup? Were her large brown eyes properly accented? Did her smile look natural? Her skin was freshly tanned, no unsightly pimples, which made her glad. She had tied back her long brown hair, but now she wished she had let it fall loose. It looked better that way, Jeff always said.

Jeff.

The thought of her boyfriend derailed her train of thought. For a fraction of a second she felt as though she had been unfaithful. She glanced away from Doug self-consciously.

He tipped a finger against his brow as a farewell. "If there's anything I can do to help . . ."

Mrs. Kottler guided Elizabeth onto a patio outside the recreation room. It was congested with plants and flowers of all kinds. A man in a wheelchair was pruning the plants, meticulously spraying the leaves and wiping them with a water bottle. He had long gray hair that poured out from under a large baseball cap. Beneath the brim of the cap he wore sunglasses so dark that she couldn't see his eyes at all. A bushy mustache and beard followed downward. It struck Elizabeth that, apart from his cheeks, his face couldn't be seen at all. He wore a baggy jogging suit that made her think he must be roasting inside.

Mrs. Kottler introduced him as Mr. Betterman, a new resident. He grunted and held a carnation out to her.

"He wants you to take it," Mrs. Kottler whispered.

Elizabeth crossed the patio to the curious-looking man and reached out to take the flower. For a second he didn't let go, but merely said with a half-smile, "I know who you are" and turned away to fiddle with the planter.

Disconcerted, Elizabeth joined Mrs. Kottler again, and they walked inside. She didn't say so, but something about the half-smile and the voice seemed familiar to her. . . .